U0093967

# 幻金天騎

## GOLDEN SKYRIDER

## 尋找神秘的呼喚者

### THE SEARCH FOR THE MYSTERIOUS CALLER

**Vera Martin** 著 ／ 李政鴻 策劃

# 策劃者的話

　　我畢業於當年北區聯招倒數第二名的私立蘭陽技術學院，而英文更是我在國中時代第一個放棄的科目。如同多數的學生一樣，我在「由你玩四年」的大學時期學無所長，因此陷入「畢業即失業」的困境，最後只得渾渾噩噩地在鐵工廠找了份勉強能餬口的工作。在毫無目標地過了一年後，才驚悟到 26K 的收入在未來難以維持一個家庭的生計。

　　大澈大悟之後，我趕緊重拾英文書本，從基礎開始苦讀。皇天不負苦心人，我的應試之路相當順利，一路過關斬將，先依序通過全民英檢初級、中級、中高級，爾後又憑藉英文優勢參加四等關務特考及三等民航特考，可謂勢如破竹。

　　英文給了我一個穩定的收入，使我不至於生活匱乏，甚至可說是改變了我的人生，我也就此明白英文的重要性。在此期勉讀者也能藉由提升英文實力，進而改善自己的生活。

策劃人　李政鴻　謹識

E-mail：li_boanerges@yahoo.com.tw

## 策劃人小檔案

◆ 91年畢業於私立復興工商專科學校
◆ 93年畢業於私立蘭陽技術學院
◆ 四等關務特考及格（英文科目90分）
◆ 三等民航特考第二名及格（英文筆試83.75分／口試84分）
◆ 全民英檢中高級及格（口說項目滿分）

# 前言

　　英文單字及文法背了又忘、忘了又背，一直是不少英文學習者的一大困擾。其實在學習英文時，背背忘忘很正常，所以需要時常拿出單字書及文法書用力複習。除了這個痛苦枯燥的辦法外，其實最輕鬆、愉快的複習方式就是透過「文章閱讀」，來使自己不斷地重複「記憶」背過的單字及文法，但這個快樂複習法一直存在策劃人的腦海裡無法實現，因為——坊間缺乏針對國中基礎單字及文法打造的文章故事（如奇幻冒險小說等）。

　　有鑑於此，策劃人特地商請外籍朋友以教育部頒布的國中兩千單字為基礎、以國中文法為核心撰寫這部奇幻冒險小說！期望國中學子能透過反覆閱讀本書輕易複習單字及文法，並同時學習翻譯。可謂全國首創、一「書」三吃！本書為作者及策劃人的嘔心瀝血之作，奇幻程度十分引人入勝，會讓人情不自禁地一讀再讀，堪稱英文學習版的《哈利波特》、《魔戒》及《暮光之城》！

　　若在閱讀本書時，在其中發現錯誤或疏漏，尚祈諸位讀者不吝來信指正。若讀者有英文學習、國家考試相關的問題，或是欲瞭解策劃人出版的講義書《別跟英語天才學國中文法（文法書）》、《別跟英語天才學國中英文（單字片語用法書）》及《國考準備及英文學習Q&A聖經》，亦歡迎各位讀者加入由策劃人創辦的FB社團「國考英文（公職國營警察高普地特國考國中英文通）」，一起提升自己的英文實力！

　　最後，在此溫馨提醒讀者：本書中文翻譯僅供學習參考之用，切勿依賴翻譯逐字逐句學習，仍以英文文意理解原意為佳。

**《本書故事純屬虛構，如有雷同實屬巧合》**

# 目錄

# List of Characters

Alfred:

The father of Johan. Alfred lives with his family in the high mountains of the Alps in Switzerland, where he was born. When he was twenty-five years old he lived next to a lake and was a fisherman. However, when the lake became too polluted he could no longer provide for his family, so he returned to the high mountains. In the mountains he is a successful salesman and able to support his family through the sales of woodwork. His forefathers have passed on the ability to talk to birds and spiders to both him and his son.

Bi Bi:

A chubby old man who is respected by the people in the village, and has the ability to travel the world in the form of a giant golden eagle at night. He is the grandson of a famous village medicine man who died at the age of ninety. Like his grandfather, he is called a 'dream catcher' and a 'golden skyrider' by the local people. When he was younger, he was a mechanic who fixed bicycles and motorcycles. He worked in the local garage and was a member of a table tennis club. Bi Bi lives in a rented Taiwanese house on a hill close to Hualien, Taiwan, ROC.

# 人物介紹

艾爾弗雷德：

　　艾爾弗雷德是約翰的父親，他出生於瑞士的阿爾卑斯高山上，直到現在他仍和家人一同住在那裡。他曾在二十五歲時搬到湖邊居住，並成為一位漁夫。但是，隨著湖泊遭受汙染，而再也無法維持家人的生計時，艾爾弗雷德又回到高山上。在山上，他是一位成功的銷售員，以銷售木製品來養活一家人。他從祖先那裡遺傳到能夠與鳥和蜘蛛對話的能力，他的兒子同時也具備這項能力。

畢畢：

　　一位身材圓潤的老人，他受到村民的敬重，在夜晚能變身成巨大的金色老鷹遨遊世界。他的祖父是村裡一位有名的藥師，在九十歲時去世。跟他的祖父一樣，當地村民都稱呼畢畢為『捕夢人』和『幻金天騎』。當他年輕時，他是一位技師，專門修理腳踏車和摩托車。他在當地車廠工作，同時也是桌球俱樂部的成員。畢畢現在住在靠近台灣花蓮山上的租屋中。

Dunkin:

The younger nephew of Bi Bi. In his youth he admired big and powerful dinosaurs and collected models as a hobby. He is tall and skinny, and loves both adventures and physical tests. He is a fit twenty-year-old who is very independent. After going to college Dunkin started training to be a sports coach in one of the senior high schools.

Dunkin lives with his elderly mother and father in one of the mountain villages near the city of Hualien in Taiwan. He is also a 'dream catcher' like his uncle and is able to change into any animal when there is danger. Besides that he has a hidden talent, which will be discovered later.

Hans:

Vincent's father, who lives in the city of Bern, Switzerland. Hans lives alone in an old brick garage, which is used for his inventions and scientific tests. Hans is a professor who has several high-level physics degrees from well-known Swiss universities and could have had the title of diplomat. Hans is totally committed to his personal projects. He has given the care of his son and daughter to his older sister and her husband who live in Bern, in an apartment building with an underground parking lot.

鄧肯：

　　畢畢較小的姪子。年輕時喜歡強壯的大恐龍，興趣是收集恐龍模型。他身材高瘦，喜愛冒險和體能訓練。他正值二十歲年紀，非常獨立。上大學以後，鄧肯開始接受訓練，希望未來能在高中擔任體育教練。

　　鄧肯跟年邁的父母住在台灣花蓮靠近山上的村落裡。他跟他的叔叔一樣，是一位『捕夢人』，而且在危險發生時，他能夠變身成任何動物。除此之外，他還有一項不為人知的才能，在日後才被發現。

漢斯：

　　文森的父親，現在住在瑞士伯恩市。漢斯獨自住在一間老舊的磚造車庫中，他在那裡進行發明研究和科學試驗。漢斯是一位擁有多個瑞士知名大學高級物理學歷的教授，原本還可能成為一位外交官。漢斯完全投入於自己的個人計畫之中。他將照顧兒子和女兒的工作託付給自己的姐姐和姐夫，他們住在位於伯恩市的一間配有地下停車場的公寓裡。

Johan:

The son of Alfred. Johan is twenty-four years old and lives with his father and mother. His mother, Mrs. Meg, is a writer and secretary who has diligently recorded all their activities and adventures.

He also has three sisters and one niece. Together they live in a wooden house, called a Swiss chalet, in the highest mountains of the Alps. He has been taught, since he was a small kid in kindergarten, to play the flute and communicate with birds and spiders.

Lia:

The friend of Yen Yen. She is a sporty eighteen-year-old girl who likes to fix problems and solve puzzles. Lia enjoys action and adventure. She has a great sense of humor while being the more practical one of the two girls. She also plays the violin and lives with her family as well as with her small pet kitten, in a home on a narrow road in Hualien, Taiwan. Lia is about to pass the final exams of senior high school.

約翰：

艾爾弗雷德的兒子。約翰現年二十四歲，與父母同住一起。他的媽媽，也就是梅格太太，是一位作家和秘書，平時會忠實地記錄下他們所有的活動和冒險事蹟。

他還有三位姐妹和一位姪女。他們全都住在阿爾卑斯山最高山峰上的一間木屋中，也就是瑞士小木屋。他從幼兒園時期就開始學吹長笛，以及與鳥和蜘蛛溝通。

莉亞：

顏顏的朋友。她是一個運動型的十八歲女孩，喜歡解決問題和破解謎團。莉亞熱愛行動及冒險。她很有幽默感，同時又是這兩個女孩中較實際的那一個。她也會拉小提琴，與家人和一隻小寵物貓住在台灣花蓮的一條小路上。莉亞即將通過高中的期末考。

Olec:

The forty-year-old dark-haired man grew up in the Russian city of Omsk. His father was a former Russian farmer who moved to the city and worked in a dirty old factory. Life was hard. Olec's family was poor and they complained bitterly. As an adult, Olec only sees greed and selfishness around him. There is neither love nor forgiveness in his life. Everyone fights for their own survival. At last, he becomes a bitter, unfeeling, negative person with an angry spirit, who believes that the world should be destroyed. This becomes his only purpose to survive. He studies engineering, chemistry and science on a university campus. Then he invents a machine, which he employs to increase violence and wars that will ruin the world's environment, and hides it in the most secure place he can think of.

Vincent:

The son of Hans the inventor. Vincent was raised by his uncle and aunt. He lives with his younger sister in an apartment building in Bern, Switzerland. His mother died of the dangerous sickness of cancer when he was four years old. He is handsome with wavy brown hair and bright blue eyes. He is short and heavy-built.

Vincent is seventeen years old and not an adult yet when he has to become a leader and take on the responsibility of saving the world, in obedience to his father's dying wish. He is intelligent and diligent. Vincent also has experience climbing the mountains close to Bern. But the duty that has to be done seems nearly impossible to him.

歐列克：

　　歐列克是一位四十歲、有著深色頭髮的男人，他從小在俄羅斯的鄂木斯克市長大。他的爸爸原本是一位俄羅斯的農夫，後來搬到城市，便在一家老舊的工廠工作。生活過得很艱辛。歐列克的家庭很貧窮，家人總是痛苦地抱怨著。長大後，歐列克在他周遭所見到的只有貪婪和自私。生活中沒有愛，也沒有寬容。每個人都為了生存而爭鬥著。到了最後，他帶著憤怒的靈魂，變成一位充滿仇恨、麻木、負面的人，認為這個世界應該被摧毀。這成為他生存的唯一目標。他在大學主修的是工程、化學和科學。他當時發明了一台時光機，用來製造暴力事件和戰爭，希望能藉此毀滅世界的環境。他將時光機藏在他能想得到最安全的地方。

文森：

　　發明家漢斯之子。文森從小由姑姑和姑丈撫養。他和妹妹一同住在瑞士伯恩市中的一間公寓裡。在他四歲時，媽媽因癌症病重而去世。他長得很英俊，有著一頭棕色波浪般的頭髮和藍色雙眼。長得不高，但身材壯碩。

　　文森現在十七歲，還未成年，但為了完成爸爸的遺願，他必須成為一位領導者，並肩負起拯救世界的責任。他很聰明，也很勤奮。文森也爬過伯恩市附近的山。但是他的使命看起來似乎是不可能完成的。

Yen Yen:

As the main character, she describes the topic of the story in her own words and adds her own opinions and feelings. Yen Yen is an eighteen-year-old slim-built girl with big eyes. She is the only daughter of parents who are famous musicians. She plays several musical instruments such as the guitar and the piano. Her father plays the trumpet. Together they live in a fancy house in the countryside, right outside of Hualien, Taiwan.

Her birthday is at the end of August and she was born in the year of the sheep. Yen Yen and Lia are classmates and their friendship has lasted for quite a few years. Yen Yen is usually less confident and social than Lia, who is more talkative, but she is soft-hearted and sincerely cares for the people around her. She cares for both the people she knows and the ones she is yet to meet.

顏顏：

　　是本故事的主角，她用自己的文字寫出故事主題，並加入自己的意見和感受。顏顏現在十八歲，身材纖細，有著一雙大眼睛。她是獨生女，爸爸媽媽都是有名的音樂家。她會彈好幾種樂器，例如吉他和鋼琴。她的爸爸會吹小喇叭。他們一家人就住在台灣花蓮郊區的一間豪華的房子裡。

　　她的生日在八月底，她是屬羊的。顏顏和莉亞是同班同學，已經認識好幾年了。莉亞比較健談，顏顏通常表現得沒有像莉亞那麼有自信，也較不擅長社交，但是顏顏是一個善良的人，真心關心她周遭的每個人。她關心她認識的人，也關心不認識的人。

# What can we do?

"Again!" I yelled, as I stood in the doorway of my friend's house on the narrow road in Hualien, Taiwan. "It has happened again. I dreamed of a big red balloon that broke when I touched it with my fingernail and out flew a small rectangular brown piece of paper that said, **'Come, I need help!'** " I don't usually remember my minor dreams, but during the last two weeks of September I had this special dream almost every night. This dream was not because I was overtired or ate the wrong food. "Lia, we really need to do something! It looks like someone is in trouble. We might be that person's only hope."

My friend Lia, a short and sporty eighteen-year-old girl with pretty long black hair and a round face, said with a smile, "Yen Yen, this happens a lot. It is like a pattern. It must have been the fourth or fifth time you told me you had that dream in the last two weeks!"

I paused to take off my socks and shoes, and put on some indoor slippers. Then I explained further by saying, "This is not like other dreams, I feel a calling in my soul telling me to take action. What if someone really needs my help and is trying to talk to me in my sleep?"

My friend has always been the one who likes adventure and action. She is a creative thinker who searches for new ways to find answers to problems, puzzles and quizzes. "But how can we find the red balloon and the person who needs help if we don't know where to start looking, Lia?" I wondered while playing with the buttons on my shirt, which was one of my habits when not being sure how to solve a problem. "This is not the time to be lazy. Something must be done about this and it must be done soon!" I emphasized in a dramatic manner, before Lia could answer me.

# 我們該怎麼辦？

　　「又來了！」我站在朋友家門口前大叫著，她的家位在台灣花蓮的小路上。「又發生了。我又夢到一顆紅色的大氣球，在接觸到我的指甲的時候破掉了，從裡面掉出一小張長方形的褐色紙條，上面寫著：『**快來，我需要幫助！**』」我通常都不會記得做過的夢，但是在九月的過去兩週，我幾乎每天晚上都夢到這個特別的夢。這個夢並不是因為我太累了，或是吃了壞掉的食物才出現的。「莉亞，我們真的需要想點辦法！這看起來像是有人有麻煩了。我們可能是這個人的唯一希望。」

　　我的朋友莉亞是一位身材嬌小、喜愛運動的十八歲女孩，她有著美麗的黑色長髮和圓臉，她笑著說：「顏顏，這經常發生，已經變成一種模式了。這兩週以來，妳已經是第四次或第五次告訴我妳做過這個同樣的夢了！」

　　我停下腳步脫掉我的襪子和鞋子，然後換上室內拖鞋。接著我進一步解釋：「這不像其他的夢，我感覺靈魂深處有人在呼喚我，要我採取行動。要是真的有人需要我的幫助，並嘗試著在我的夢中跟我對話呢？」

　　我的朋友是個喜歡冒險和行動的人。她有創新的思考模式，總是嘗試用新的方式解決問題、謎題和測驗。「但是，如果我們不知道該從哪裡找起，要如何找到那個紅色氣球，和那個需要幫助的人呢，莉亞？」我一邊詢問著，一邊把玩著襯衫上的鈕扣，這是我不確定該怎麼解決問題時會出現的習慣動作。「現在不是懶惰的時候。我們一定要處理這件事，而且一定要盡快！」在莉亞回答我的問題之前，我用誇張的語調強調著。

"There is a chubby old man who lives on the top of a hill close to my house," said Lia. "I heard the neighbors talk about him. They say he is a 'dream catcher' as well as a 'golden skyrider' and lives all alone. Even though he is well-known and respected in the local village, he seldom goes out now. It is said that he knows about dreams and ghosts. In the last century his grandfather was a village medicine man and a vendor of medicinal plants."

I remembered his name being quietly spoken in the town. "I think it is Bi Bi. His house is not far away, just across the modern highway bridge. It is Saturday morning. Maybe we should go visit him, because many people go to him for advice. Let's go and see him now!" I said loudly into Lia's ear as if underlining every word. "Let's go, let's go, the person who wrote the note and put it into the balloon may be in danger!"

After listening to me, Bi Bi nodded his head while thinking deeply. "Yes, yes," he finally said, "a person is calling for help in your dream, but you need to tell me more."

I slowly started talking as I was trying to remember what I saw in my dreams, "Well... it could be in another country. I saw some mountains but they looked different from the mountains in Taiwan. They were not familiar at all. No trees and plants, only black and gray rocks covered with snow. It looked cold and empty." I suddenly thought of the last dream. "*There was a waterfall and, later in the dream, the big red balloon was hanging out of the window of an apartment building next to the bridge that was built by a rich dishonest businessman, and I was wearing a long black coat with a hood that covered my head. How strange...*"

「我家附近的山上住著一個身材圓潤的男性長者，」莉亞說著。「我聽過鄰居談論他。他們說他是一位『捕夢人』，同時也是一位『幻金天騎』，且他獨自深居。雖然他很有名，也受當地村民的敬重，但是他很少外出。據說他瞭解夢和鬼魂。他的祖父在上個世紀是村裡的一位藥師和藥草商。」

我記得鎮上的人都私下討論著他。「我想是畢畢。他的家離這裡不遠，就在現代化公路橋的那端。現在是星期六早上，也許我們應該去拜訪他，有很多人都是為了得到一些建議而去拜訪他。我們現在就去找他！」我大聲地對著莉亞的耳朵說，好像在強調每個字一般。「我們走，我們走，寫紙條並把它放在氣球裡的那個人，也許正面臨著危險！」

聽完我的夢境之後，畢畢陷入沉思，並點著頭。「是的，是的，」他總算開口說話，「有個人正在妳的夢中呼喚求救，但是妳還得告訴我更多才行。」

我試著回憶我在夢裡見到的事情，並開始慢慢地訴說著，「嗯……地點可能位於另一個國家。我看到一些山，但看起來不像台灣的山，一點都不像。那裡沒有任何的樹木或植物，只有覆蓋著白雪的黑色和灰色岩石。那裡看起來很冷、很空曠。」我突然間想到最後一個夢。「那裡有一個瀑布，在夢的後半段，那個紅色的大氣球懸浮在一間公寓建築的窗外，旁邊有一座橋，那座橋是由一位沒有誠信的富商出錢蓋的，我穿著一件黑色連帽長大衣，並戴著大衣帽子。多奇怪啊……」

Bi Bi closed his eyes and slowly started moving from side to side while standing in the dark section of the living room on the second floor of his house. He was listening to soft classical style music, which was playing on the cassette player. The sun had gone down about one hour ago. The moon and the stars, like bright dots in the sky, had appeared to shine their soft light through the window. "Mountains and waterfalls," said Bi Bi softly again and again. "Did you see any stars or distant planets in your dreams?"

"I don't think so," I answered being a little confused. Bi Bi had not told us that his grandfather was known as the 'dream catcher' with the gift of understanding ghosts, languages and explaining dreams. Bi Bi had spent his sleeping hours traveling the world as a 'golden skyrider' from the deepest cave to the highest mountain, in the form of a giant golden eagle. At times he had even gone into outer space to see the beauty of the universe.

Bi Bi looked at me by the light of the candle, which was burning in his living room and said kindly, "Yen Yen, for one week I would like you to get into the habit of going to bed every night before 10 o'clock p.m., after you drink a glass of warm milk and eat some cookies or maybe a banana. It will help you feel lazy and your sleep will be deep. It will be useful because you may have dreams that will show us what our next step should be." He paused and said sincerely, "Hop to bed and more will be shown!"

　　畢畢站在二樓客廳的陰暗處，闔上雙眼，開始緩慢地來回踱步。他正聽著從卡帶錄音機中播放的柔和古典樂。太陽大約在一個小時前下山。月亮和星星就像天空中的光點般點綴在天邊，透過窗戶閃耀著柔和的光線。「群山和瀑布，」畢畢輕聲地反覆說著：「妳在夢中有看到任何星星或遙遠的星球嗎？」

　　「我覺得應該沒有，」我困惑地回答道。畢畢沒有告訴我們，他的祖父是大家所稱的『捕夢人』，擁有能夠理解鬼魂、語言和解釋夢境的天賦。畢畢在睡覺時會化身為『幻金天騎』，以一隻巨大金色老鷹的姿態遨遊世界，從最深處的洞穴到最高聳的山脈，他都去過。有時候，他甚至會飛到外太空，欣賞宇宙之美。

　　畢畢的客廳點著燭火，他透過燭光看向我，和藹地說：「顏顏，我希望妳接下來的一個星期能養成每天晚上十點前上床睡覺的習慣，並在睡覺前喝一杯溫熱的牛奶、吃些餅乾，或是一根香蕉。這會幫助妳放鬆，而且能讓妳睡得更熟。這會為我們帶來幫助，因為妳的夢將會告訴我們下一步該怎麼做。」他停頓一下，接著真誠地說：「上床睡覺吧，你會得到更多答案的！」

# Feathers, feathers, feathers

Lia woke up with a shock when her cellphone, which she usually put next to her purse on the bookcase by her bed, suddenly started ringing loudly at three o'clock in the early morning. Sleepily she opened the curtains and looked out of the window. The stars were still bright marks in the sky and the moon was hiding behind some clouds.

"Lia, Lia!" A voice excitedly sounded in Lia's ear as soon as she answered the phone. "I saw feathers, feathers in all shapes, colors and sizes slowly falling from the sky. Then the red rubber balloon burst and the brown rectangular piece of paper landed on my arm."

"Yen Yen, do you know what time it is? You woke me up almost in the middle of the night. What do you mean 'feathers'?" Lia slowly opened her eyes wide and imagined feathers floating down. She thought to herself, "Should we assume those objects are really feathers? Did the feathers come from birds?" Too sleepy to think clearly, all she could say was, "Yen Yen, go back to sleep, don't call me again tonight. We will talk about it in the morning!"

Almost a year before my dream about the feathers, in a far away country, a twenty-four-year-old, named Johan, looked up at the sky with watchful eyes. The sun broke through a mass of clouds and brightened the view for a short period. He was standing on top of one of the highest mountains in Switzerland. "Now is the time," he thought to himself excitedly, "at last the time has come to send out the call. It is time for the yearly meeting!"

# 羽毛、羽毛、各種羽毛

半夜三點半，莉亞的手機突然大聲響起，她的手機通常放在床邊書架上的包包旁邊，莉亞因此驚醒過來。睡眼惺忪的她拉開窗簾，看向窗外。星星仍然在天空中明亮地閃耀著，而月亮正躲在雲層後面。

「莉亞、莉亞！」接起手機後，一個興奮的聲音在莉亞耳邊響起。「我看到一堆羽毛，各種不同形狀、顏色和大小的羽毛從天空中緩緩飄落。然後那個紅色橡膠氣球突然破掉，長方形的褐色紙條就落到我的手臂上。」

「顏顏，妳知道現在幾點了嗎？妳在大半夜把我吵醒。妳說的『羽毛』是指什麼？」莉亞慢慢地睜開雙眼，想像著羽毛飄浮落下的樣子。她想著：「我們是否該認為這些東西是真的羽毛？這些羽毛是鳥的羽毛嗎？」莉亞太睏了，無法清楚地思考，她現在能說的只是：「顏顏，回去睡覺，今晚不要再打給我，我們早上再談這件事！」

大約在我夢見羽毛的一年前，在遙遠的國家，有一位二十四歲、名為約翰的男人，正抬頭警惕地注視著天空。太陽從雲層中破曉而出，短暫地照亮了大地上的所有景物。他正站在瑞士最高峰的山頂上。「時候到了，」他興奮地想著，「終於是時候發出呼喚了。年度大會的時間到了！」

Johan had jumped out of bed early this morning to put on the pants, belt and shirt that his father had lent him for this special day. He dressed himself slowly and carefully.

He thought back to his early childhood when he was just a small seven-year-old boy with a childlike smile, who was happy to climb the mountain with his father. His father, Alfred, had prepared him for this event from the time of his birth by modeling what to do. For many hours Johan had followed his dad's example, by holding the simple wooden flute with his thumb and fingers. With shaking hands, Johan had been learning how to pipe the magical music that would call the flock of colorful birds from all parts of the country for the yearly meeting.

As Johan lifted the flute to his mouth he slowly thought the words that would give power to the call, "Fly, fly now with all your might. Fly, fly now to change a life. Your feathers will guide the person who will come to help the one who will save the world." The excitement of the moment made him ignore the freezing cold wind that felt like needles on his skin. "This is the reason why I have been practicing my whole life!" he thought bright-eyed.

For many years the birds had painfully pulled out their feathers and had let them gently float to the ground. But nothing had been gained by this, no help had come. "But this year, this year... " Johan felt new energy moving through his body. "Would the person being called accept it, listen and understand?" Somehow it felt like the perfect time and place. Johan was satisfied and whispered more magical words, "Joy comes in the morning."

約翰今天一大早就從床上跳起，穿上褲子與襯衫，並繫上皮帶，這些都是爸爸特別借給他，專門要在今天這樣特殊的日子穿的。他緩慢且慎重地著衣整裝。

他回想起兒童時期，當時他只是一個七歲的小男孩，帶著童稚的笑容，開心地與爸爸一起登山。他的父親，艾爾弗雷德，從他出生的那一天起就開始為這件事做準備，他示範該做的事給約翰看，讓他能夠迎接這件大事。很多時候，約翰跟著爸爸的示範，以手指和大拇指握著簡單的木製長笛。藉由舞動雙手手指，約翰習得如何吹出具有魔法的音樂，召喚五顏六色的鳥群從全國各地飛來參加年度大會。

約翰將長笛靠近嘴邊，心裡慢慢想著能賦予召喚力量的咒語，「飛吧，現在盡全力飛翔。飛吧，為改變生命而飛吧。你的羽毛將會指引那個前來幫助救世主的人。」這個時刻是那麼令人興奮，使得約翰絲毫不在意像許多細針扎在皮膚上一般的刺骨寒風。「這正是我這一生不斷練習的原因！」他眼神發亮地想著。

多年至今，鳥群痛苦地拔下牠們的羽毛，讓羽毛緩緩地飄落在地。但是這麼做卻未有所獲，沒有任何幫助出現。「但是今年，今年……」約翰感覺到一股新能量流經全身。「接收到呼喚的那個人會接受、傾聽，然後理解嗎？」不知為何，他感覺現在正是完美的時間和地點。約翰感到很滿意，然後輕聲地說出更多咒語：「喜悅於早晨到來。」

Bi Bi was quietly sitting in his tiny Taiwanese house, going through his box of stationery and looking at an old photo album full of photos taken with his well-used camera. He was smiling contently as he heard Lia and I discussing the falling feathers. He brushed his fingers through his hair as a gesture of happiness. He knew about these feathers. Several years ago he had explored the Swiss mountains in his dreams, flying above the clouds with the power of the mighty wings of the golden eagle. He had seen the feathers fall to indicate a special place in the mountains. But he had heard the call without understanding the meaning.

He stood up to turn on the fan as the room was becoming uncomfortably hot and humid. The level of the temperature improved right away. Then he reached for his old-fashioned house phone and dialled the telephone number of the nearby restaurant to ask them to deliver some dinner. After all of us had finished eating, Bi Bi added some powdered milk to his tea and thought, "It is true, the dreams are real! It has something to do with Yen Yen. Is she the one being called?"

# Dreaming juice and memories

"What does it mean?" I said impatiently and a little rudely. I put both my hands on my waist and continued, "Feathers, feathers... I love feathers. I love birds. I would like to collect the nice colorful feathers I saw, even the gray feathers of a pigeon. But whose feathers are they? What does that have to do with a rubber balloon that is red or a person needing help?" I looked at Bi Bi, who was sitting in the shadows, in the far corner of his small untidy living room, on an uncomfortable small stool.

畢畢安靜地坐在他的台式小屋內，仔細翻找一箱裝滿文具的箱子，凝視著一本舊相簿，裡面放滿了以他那台好用的相機所拍攝的照片。當他聽到我和莉亞討論飄落的羽毛時，臉上露出了滿足的笑容。他用指尖梳過頭髮，舉手投足間充滿喜悅。他知道這些羽毛。幾年前，他曾在夢中探索過瑞士的山脈，利用金色老鷹巨翅的力量飛越雲層。他曾看過羽毛飄落的方向都指向著群山中一個特別的地方。他也曾經聽過那個呼喚，但當時還不了解其中的意義。

房間開始變得越來越熱且潮濕，讓人感到不舒服。他站起身，打開了電扇，房間的溫度立即降了下來。接著，他拿起屋子裡老式的室內電話，撥給附近的餐廳，請他們外送晚餐。當大家都吃完晚餐後，畢畢在茶裡加入一些奶粉，想著：「是真的，這些夢都是真的！這些都與顏顏有關。她是那個被呼喚的人嗎？」

# 引夢藥與回憶

「這代表什麼意思？」我不耐煩地問道，口氣甚至有些無禮。我把雙手插在腰上，繼續說著：「羽毛、羽毛……我愛羽毛，我愛鳥。我會想要蒐集我看到的那些美麗且五彩繽紛的羽毛，甚至是鴿子的灰色羽毛。但是那些羽毛是誰的呢？這些羽毛和紅色橡皮氣球或需要幫助的人之間，又有什麼關聯呢？」我望向畢畢，他正坐在遠處的角落陰影裡，在他又小又凌亂的客廳中，坐在一張看起來不是很舒服的小凳子上。

"I have no idea," he said humbly with a quiet voice. "But it seems to be in another country for sure." Bi Bi was silent for a moment, at last he said, "I wonder what the root of the problem is. It seems the trouble has already been expected for a long time. Perhaps... only one special person can answer the call."

Suddenly Bi Bi stood up and walked across the room, opening the door to the basement of his little house as if he was trying to get something. But then he turned around and said, "Yen Yen, what was actually written on the piece of paper in your dream? Do you remember that small piece of brown paper that fell on your arm when the balloon popped? Was the paper blank on the other side? Was there any trace of anything else on the note? It could have been almost unseen like it had been erased."

I closed my eyelids trying to recall my dreams. "Hmm... no, I didn't see anything. Just the message, **'Come, I need help!'** It was written with big letters on the dirty brown paper. Not with a pencil or a pen, perhaps with a black rock or a crayon."

"Drink more warm milk at night," laughed Lia while she was taking out her contact lenses and putting on glasses. "Sweet dreams tonight, answers for tomorrow!"

Bi Bi agreed with her with half a smile. Then he reached for a small bottle with a dark green liquid, which was almost completely hidden under a pile of old, printed newspapers. "Drink this; it is a well-known ancient herbal drink. Common people of all ages have named it 'dreaming juice'. If you add some lemon it will taste better and your body will be able to use it more easily."

「我不知道，」他用平靜的語氣低聲地說。「但幾乎可以肯定的是，這發生在另一個國家。」畢畢沉默了一會兒，最後他說：「我在想問題的根源是什麼。似乎這個問題存在已久。或許……只有一個特別的人才能回應這個呼喚。」

突然間，畢畢站起身，走過房間，打開小屋內通往地下室的門，看起來像是要拿什麼東西。但是，接下來他轉過身問：「顏顏，你夢中的那張紙條上究竟寫著什麼？你還記得氣球破掉時，那張落在妳手臂上的褐色紙條嗎？那張紙條的背面是空白的嗎？紙條上是否還有其他線索？這些線索可能幾乎看不見，就像是字跡被擦掉一般。」

我閉上雙眼，試著回想那些夢。「嗯……我沒有看見其他內容。只有那個訊息，『**快來，我需要幫助！**』這幾個大大的字寫在那張髒兮兮的褐色紙條上。不是用鉛筆或原子筆寫的，也許是用黑色岩石或蠟筆寫的。」

「睡前多喝一些溫牛奶吧，」莉亞一邊取下隱形眼鏡，換上眼鏡，一邊大笑著說。「祝妳今晚有個好夢，明天就能找到答案！」

畢畢似笑非笑地同意莉亞的話。然後他拿來一個裝滿深綠色液體的小瓶子，這個小瓶子幾乎完全被一疊舊報紙給掩蓋了。「喝下這個；這是非常有名的古藥草茶，一般人稱它為『引夢藥』。加入一點檸檬，它的味道會好些，而且能發揮更大的作用。」

Lia added jokingly, "If you have a sweet tooth you can even put some sugar in it or eat some candy! But you may get a toothache from eating too much candy and have to go to the dentist."

After Bi Bi finished repairing his door, which wouldn't close the right way, and washed his trousers and underwear, he became more serious and said, "You will be able to describe what happens in the dreams more clearly and you will still remember them in the morning. Be careful; drink it slowly right before you go to sleep." Then he emphasized, "And don't drink too much or you will wake up as early as five o'clock in the morning with a big headache."

I was unsure if I should drink the unknown green liquid that Bi Bi had offered to me. "How would this affect my health and my body?" I considered. I had read books where either magical spells or strange mixtures changed normal people into violent monsters or ugly animals.

"I am scared this drink will make me swell up like a blowfish and then I will pop like the balloon!" I took out my silver earrings to get ready for bed but first I picked up my cellphone. Lia would have some helpful advice. Last month Lia had been in the hospital to see a doctor after sitting on an anthill in the park. She had been quite upset with those naughty bugs. She had so many ant bites she almost looked like a blowfish. "Lia, are you sleeping?" I asked shyly.

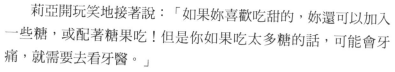

　　莉亞開玩笑地接著說：「如果妳喜歡吃甜的，妳還可以加入一些糖，或配著糖果吃！但是你如果吃太多糖的話，可能會牙痛，就需要去看牙醫。」

　　畢畢修完那扇關不攏的門之後，開始清洗他的長褲和內衣褲，並以非常嚴肅的表情說道：「妳將能更清楚地描述出夢裡發生的事，而且醒來後也能記住這些事。但要注意的是；你要在上床睡覺前慢慢喝下它。」接著，他強調地說著：「不要喝太多，不然妳會在凌晨五點就醒來，而且頭會非常痛。」

　　我不確定我是否應該喝下畢畢給我的這個不知名的綠色液體。「它會不會影響我的健康和身體呢？」我想著。我曾讀過一些書，書上說有些咒語或是奇怪的飲料會把正常人變成狂暴的怪物，或是醜陋的動物。

　　「我很擔心這個飲料會讓我膨脹，變得像隻河豚一樣，然後我會像那顆氣球一樣爆掉！」我摘下我的銀製耳環，準備上床睡覺，但是，我先拿起了我的手機。莉亞應該可以給我一些有用的建議。上個月，莉亞因為在公園不小心坐到一個蟻丘上而去醫院看醫生。她對那些討厭的蟲子感到厭惡。她全身都被螞蟻咬，腫起來的樣子看起來幾乎就像隻河豚。「莉亞，妳睡了嗎？」我不好意思地問著。

Lia looked at the watch on her wrist and said, "What's the matter? You must enjoy waking me up by calling me in the middle of the night." Then she said with a laugh, "Well, are you worried your hair will turn green or your nose will grow big? Or that you will turn into a pumpkin or a wolf? Don't you know that Bi Bi is a gentleman? He would never give you anything that would hurt you. Come on, Yen Yen, you are thinking too much! The drink is made from vegetables, it is like tea. Don't you drink tea every afternoon and eat a bowl of cereal every morning? Stop worrying and swallow it now, nothing will go wrong!"

# Hidden directions

That evening, when the sun was setting, Bi Bi felt free as a bird. "I am blessed to be able to fly like this," he thought to himself. In the form of the mighty magical golden eagle he could fly at high speed above the cities, forests, rivers and valleys. At that height he could see a long distance. The primary reason that he was going out was to go back to the place where he had first seen the feathers several years ago.

His attention was suddenly drawn to the sound of rushing waterfalls pouring down the mountains at fast speed. "I cannot see the water!" he said surprised. "That is impossible, because I know that sound!"

莉亞看著手上的錶，邊說著：「怎麼了？妳真的很喜歡在大半夜打電話吵醒我。」然後她笑著說：「好吧，妳是不是擔心妳的頭髮會變成綠色的，或是鼻子會變大？或者妳會變成一顆南瓜或一匹狼？妳不知道畢畢是一位紳士嗎？他絕不會給妳任何會傷害妳的東西。拜託，顏顏，妳想太多了！那個飲料是植物製成的，就像茶一樣。妳不是每天下午都會喝一杯茶、每天早上都會吃一碗麥片嗎？別擔心了，現在就吞下它吧，不會出差錯的！」

# 隱藏的方向

那天晚上，當太陽下山以後，畢畢化身成一隻鳥類，感受著自由，牠自顧自地想著：「我一定是受到眷顧，才能像現在這樣翱翔著。」以神奇的金色巨鷹之姿，牠能夠高速飛過城市、森林、河流和山谷。在那樣的高度，牠能夠看得非常遠。牠此次飛翔的主要原因，是為了回到多年前第一次見到那些羽毛的地方。

突然間，牠的注意力被山間傾瀉而下的瀑布水聲吸引。「我沒有看到瀑布的水！」牠驚訝地說著。「這是不可能的，因為我記得那種聲音！」

Bi Bi flew down to see a group of mountains, also called a mountain range. He used his sharp eyes to observe the area more closely. On the way he saw horse riders on a narrow mountain road enjoying the peaceful scenery and a beautiful rainbow that had appeared after a rainstorm. Finally he detected the entrance of a man-made tunnel on the steep side of a mountain, close to several lakes. "I would like to discover more, is that tunnel really man-made? That is very clever. In the last fifty years there has been no limit to what man can build," he said thoughtfully to himself. "Or could it have been made by a strong rush of water over many centuries, which has dried up?"

"On the other hand, there could be thousands of tunnels in this mountain range and it would take too much time to check them all. My goal is to stay here till the sunrise, in this foreign country, to gather more information. In the sunlight I may notice more." The giant eagle found a place to rest on the dry straw behind a big rock, which felt like a comfy nest. He tucked his head into his feathers to try to stay warm at a temperature of seven degrees and closed his weary eyes. "There is always hope for tomorrow," was his last thought before he fell asleep.

"What, what?" Bi Bi felt something landing on his black eagle beak. "That is not snow. It is not freezing like snow. But it is light and soft!"

As he opened his brown eagle eyes uncertainly Bi Bi realized it was a nice-looking feather. Colorful feathers were falling down all around him and on the nearest mountain of the mountain range.

　　畢畢向下飛，看到了連綿的山峰，也稱作一條山脈。牠用牠敏銳的雙眼，更仔細地觀察著那個區域。一路上，牠看見狹窄的山路上有人正騎著馬，享受著寧靜的風景，以及在暴風雨後出現的那道美麗彩虹。最後，牠發現一個人造隧道的入口，就在其中一座山較陡峭的那一側，附近有好幾個湖泊。「我想要知道更多，那個隧道真的是人造的嗎？那真是非常聰明。在過去五十年來，幾乎已經沒有什麼東西是人類無法建造的。」牠陷入沉思後說著。「或者這是由一道強勁的水流，在幾世紀間不斷沖刷而成的，如今這道水流已經乾涸了？」

　　「另一方面，這座山脈可能有數千個隧道，要全部探查過會花太長的時間。我的目標是待在這裡直到天亮，以便蒐集更多資訊。在陽光照射下，我應該能注意到更多東西。」這隻巨鷹在一顆大岩石後方找到一個休息地點，牠停在一堆乾草上，這個乾草堆就像是一個舒適的鳥巢。牠把頭埋進羽毛中，試著在七度低溫中保持溫暖，然後牠閉上疲憊的雙眼。「明日總會出現希望。」是牠入睡前的最後想法。

　　「什麼，什麼？」畢畢感覺到有東西落在牠的黑色鷹喙上。「那不是雪。不像是凍結的雪。這東西很輕、很軟！」

　　當牠猶疑地睜開褐色的鷹眼時，畢畢發現，這是一根美麗的羽毛。五顏六色的羽毛飄落在牠的周圍以及山脈間離牠最近的一座山峰上。

"The feathers! I know, I know! I have seen them before. Yen Yen has dreamed about them. And a waterfall... This must be the place that the feathers are calling her to!" Bi Bi spread his wings and was soon flying above the clouds, going towards the Taiwanese east coast. "This is welcome news, this is welcome news!" he repeated out loud.

At the same time, about eight o'clock on Wednesday morning, I first fed my two puppies from a small saucer and paid my Internet bill in the modern shopping mall. Then I happily jogged to Lia's house while listening to my walkman tape recorder. I felt the pleasant breeze blowing through my hair and the sun warming my back. I was wearing my summer clothes, a comfortable sports skirt and top, which were suitable for exercise. On the way I could see young children, with their mother, excitedly flying kites in the park. This day was going to be wonderful. I could feel it in my bones.

When I woke up this morning and was brushing my teeth, last night's dream came to mind as clearly as going to a movie theater and watching the dream. It was as if actors and actresses were acting in a movie on the screen. It was almost like the cowboy film I watched the other day. "It was so cool. It must have been the dreaming juice!" I said cheerfully. Then I turned on my fan and quickly ran to the mirror. "Is my nose bigger? Do I look like a wolf? Have my legs, stomach and shoulders become swollen like a blue blowfish?" I was a little worried till I looked in the mirror and said out loud, "Great, I still look like myself, and no headache. I am a lucky girl!"

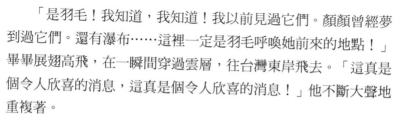

「是羽毛！我知道，我知道！我以前見過它們。顏顏曾經夢到過它們。還有瀑布……這裡一定是羽毛呼喚她前來的地點！」畢畢展翅高飛，在一瞬間穿過雲層，往台灣東岸飛去。「這真是個令人欣喜的消息，這真是個令人欣喜的消息！」他不斷大聲地重複著。

就在週三大概早上八點鐘的時候，我先用小碟子餵食我的兩隻小狗，然後前往現代化的購物中心繳我的網路帳單。之後，我一邊聽著卡帶隨身聽，一邊開心地慢跑到莉亞的家，感受著舒服的微風拂過我的髮梢，溫暖的太陽照耀著我的背部。我穿著夏季的服裝，一條舒適的運動裙和一件上衣，是一套非常適合運動的裝扮。途中，我看到媽媽帶著小孩子，在公園興奮地放風箏。今天一定會是很棒的一天。我打從內心相信著。

當我今天早上起床刷牙時，昨夜的夢境鮮明地在腦海裡出現，畫面就像是去電影院看電影一般清晰，螢幕中的男女演員賣力地表演著。這感覺就像我前幾天看的一部牛仔電影一樣真實。「真是太酷了。一定是引夢藥的緣故！」我歡喜地說著。然後，我打開電扇，迅速地跑向鏡子。「我的鼻子有沒有變大？我會不會看起來像一匹狼？我的腿、胃和肩膀有沒有像隻藍色的河豚一樣腫起來？」我有點擔心，直到我跑到鏡子前，大叫著：「太好了，我還是原來的自己，而且完全沒有頭痛。我真是個幸運的女孩！」

"Yen Yen, it is so good to see you!" Lia greeted me at the door by giving me a big hug. She must have just stepped out of her bed because her bed sheets were hanging off her bed and she was still wearing her pair of pajamas. Her hair was sticking out in all directions. "Don't mind the way I look, I just rolled out of bed! After breakfast I will wash my hair and use a hairdryer to dry it or I may go to a hairdresser," she laughed.

"Would you like some breakfast or an early lunch, like a brunch?" Lia said with a sleepy face. "I have three grams of ham, a dozen eggs, tomato ketchup, a kilogram of strawberries with cream, a loaf of bread and a liter of orange juice, unless you would rather eat some fried rice with pork, spring onions and cabbage. I also have a big watermelon. Here are some chopsticks, salt and pepper to put on the table."

She sounded like a waitress or a manager of a restaurant but I was too excited to even think about food. I knew Lia did not eat yet so I decided to be patient. "Whatever you are going to eat sounds good to me," I answered. 'Clang, clang, stomp, stomp.' Strange noises were coming out of the kitchen as Lia pulled out woks, pans and plates to cook whatever she felt like eating.

Then I heard her say, "Oh, too bad I do not have any more flour. I will need to cook something else on the stove!"

I felt my patience had run out, "Are you done cooking food yet?" I could not wait any longer, I felt like exploding and popping like the balloon if I could not tell her right away what I had found out.

"Lia, I found out something else in my dream last night!" I finally yelled across the dining room to the kitchen.

「顏顏，真高興看到妳！」莉亞站在門邊給我一個大大的擁抱當作招呼。她一定才剛起床，因為她的床單從床上垂下來，而且她還穿著睡衣。她的頭髮凌亂不堪。「別介意我的樣子，我才剛起床呢！吃完早餐後我會洗頭，然後用吹風機吹乾，或是去美髮店，」她笑著說。

「妳想不想吃些早餐，或是把早餐當午餐吃，像是早午餐？」莉亞睡眼惺忪地說。「我有三公克的火腿、一打雞蛋、番茄醬、一公斤的草莓和奶油、一條土司和一公升的柳橙汁，還是妳會想吃豬肉炒飯，我會加些洋蔥和高麗菜進去。我還有一顆大西瓜。這裡有幾雙筷子、鹽和胡椒粉，拿去放在桌上。」

她的口氣聽起來就像是女服務生或是餐廳經理，但是我太興奮了，無暇去思考食物的問題。我知道莉亞還沒有吃過東西，所以我決定耐心等她吃完餐點。「不管妳要吃什麼，我都好。」我回答她。「噹啷、噹啷、碰、碰。」奇怪的聲音從廚房傳出，莉亞拿出炒菜鍋、平底鍋和盤子，要煮些不知道是什麼、反正就是她想吃的東西。

接著，我聽到她說：「噢，太可惜了，我的麵粉不夠。我得煮其他的東西！」

我感覺到我的耐心已經用盡，「妳煮完了沒？」我已經等不及了，如果不能馬上告訴她我發現的事情，我覺得我會像夢中的氣球一樣爆掉。

「莉亞，我昨晚在夢裡發現了其他事情！」我忍不住從飯廳的另一端朝廚房的方向大喊。

Lia's head appeared in the hallway. "What?" she asked curiously.

"Well... Bi Bi was right, there was something else written on the small piece of paper," I replied. "In the first part of my dream, *I was on my way back home from the department store and was standing by the side of the road waiting for a truck to pass, when it started raining. I had the note, out of the red balloon, in my hand. I didn't have an umbrella so the brown piece of paper got wet. To my surprise several very small words slowly became visible. It said, 'Follow the red deer.' It seemed the paper and the ink were especially designed to hide the message when it was dry. Because when the paper dried up, the words disappeared.*"

Lia stopped eating, put her fork, spoon and knife down and cleaned her mouth with a napkin. Then she said with emotion in her voice, "Let's go visit Bi Bi now!"

"Wait, wait, not so fast!" I jumped out of the comfortable armchair and blocked the door. "I have much more to tell you. I didn't describe the second part of the dream yet."

莉亞探出頭。她好奇地問：「什麼事？」

「這個嘛……畢畢是對的，那張小紙條上還寫著其他東西。」我回答她。「在夢境的前半段，我正要從百貨公司回家，當我站在路邊等一台卡車經過時，正好開始下起小雨。從紅色氣球中飄落的那張紙條被我拿在手中。因為當時我沒有雨傘，所以那張褐色紙條濕掉了。出乎意料之外的是，一些很小的字詞逐漸浮現。上面寫著：『**跟著那頭紅色的鹿。**』那張紙條和墨水似乎經過特殊的設計，刻意要隱藏上面的訊息。因為當紙條乾掉時，那些字也跟著消失了。」

正在吃東西的莉亞停了下來，放下叉子、湯匙和刀子，用紙巾擦擦嘴巴後，語帶激動地說：「我們現在就去找畢畢！」

「等等，等等，別那麼快！」我從舒適的扶手椅上跳起，擋住門口。「我還有其他的事情要告訴妳。我還沒說這個夢的後半段呢。」

# In the apartment building

I started telling Lia about the dream, "*There was a teenage boy, walking up six flights of stairs as he followed his aunt, who was hurrying to get home. In his hand he held the most precious thing that he owned. The postal service had just sent out a mailman to deliver some mail to him. He had received a letter from his father! On the front of the letter, in big print, was his name, Vincent. Under his name was written the address of the apartment building in Bern, the city in Switzerland where he lived with his uncle and aunt on the sixth floor. 'Yes, at last, a letter from dad!' he congratulated himself. In the dream Vincent ran to catch up with his aunt, his wavy light brown hair rocking in time with his steps.*"

"*His father, Hans, was an inventor,*" I continued while sitting in the comfortable armchair. "*Hans lived in a private place in the woods, in an old brick garage that used to be a storeroom. But now the garage looked like a museum as it had become a giant locker for all his inventions. His total focus was on his work. He therefore had a sign on his front gate declaring '**no noise is allowed**'. Vincent and his younger sister had to move in with their relatives to have a normal youth as their mother had died of cancer when he was four years old, and his sister was just a one-year-old baby.*"

Then I added, "*As soon as he had finished eating his favorite sandwich with butter, cheese, beef slices, lettuce and tomato, Vincent read his dad's letter. When he was still chewing his food and quickly drinking a cup of coffee, Vincent opened the letter with his heart missing a beat. Many thoughts raced through his mind, 'What could be important enough for dad to stop his work and write me a letter? Did his tests succeed?*' "

# 那棟公寓裡

我開始向莉亞訴說夢境：「有一個少年，他的姑姑急著要回家，他跟著姑姑走上六層階梯。他的手上拿著自己最珍視的東西。郵局剛派出一位郵差送信給他。他收到來自父親的信！信封的正面大大地寫著他的名字，文森。他的名字下面寫的是位於瑞士伯恩市的公寓住址，他和姑姑、姑丈同住在六樓。『太好了，總算收到爸爸的信了！』他開心地說著。在夢中，文森用跑的跟上姑姑，他那波浪般的淺棕色頭髮隨著他的腳步上下跳動著。」

「他的父親，漢斯，是一位發明家，」我坐回舒適的扶手椅上繼續說著。「漢斯住在樹林中的隱密處，住在一間用磚塊蓋成的車庫中，那間車庫之前是一間儲藏室。不過現在這間車庫變成了一個巨大的儲物櫃，裡面放滿了他發明的所有物品。他把所有的心思都放在發明上。所以他在前門貼上一張『禁止發出噪音』的標示。在文森四歲時，由於媽媽死於癌症，文森和他的妹妹為了可以像一般的青少年一樣正常地成長，所以必須搬去和親戚一起住，當時他的妹妹還只是個一歲的小嬰兒而已。」

然後我接著說：「他一吃完他最喜歡的三明治夾奶油、起司、牛肉片、生菜和番茄後，文森開始讀父親寄來的信。他一邊咀嚼食物，一邊快速地喝著咖啡，文森打開信的時候，興奮地幾乎停止了心跳。許多想法湧上心頭：『什麼事這麼重要，讓爸爸停下工作，寫信給我？是不是他的試驗成功了？』」

I looked at Lia who was leaning forward and holding the edges of the dining table so tightly that her fingers turned white. "Go on, go on!" said Lia, eager to find out what was in the letter. "I sure hope the dream brings to light what the message means."

I said, "Ssh... I need to focus. I don't want to forget this important part."

I was silent for a moment and then continued, "*Vincent's dad wrote, 'I found it, I found it! It finally makes sense. After twenty-nine years of trying and failing, I discovered the answer at last. Son, I am too old now to do anything about it. You are young and you are brave, you have the strength to set this right. It is our duty to save the world from total ruin. Listen carefully. I cannot explain everything in this letter. Come to my place in the woods, your aunt will give you directions. Come soon, I do not have much longer to live!'*"

I stood up, hit a mosquito that had landed on my leg, and slowly walked to the kitchen sink to wash my face and hands in an attempt to come back to reality.

"And then... was there more?" said Lia with a concerned voice.

"No, I woke up because I heard someone knocking on the door. It was my brother asking if I had a can of cola leftover from my grandmother's birthday party. Then he started talking about the neighbor's babysitter, and the taxi he took to the market to buy yummy mangoes and apple pies. Too bad... " I answered.

　　我看著莉亞，莉亞身體前傾靠著餐桌，手緊握著餐桌邊緣，手指甚至因為過於用力而發白。「繼續，繼續！」莉亞急切地想知道那封信中究竟寫了些什麼。「我真切地希望這個夢能告訴我們訊息的內容是什麼。」

　　我說：「噓……我需要專心。我不想忘記這個重要的部分。」

　　我沉默了一會兒，然後繼續說道：「文森的父親寫著：『我發現了，我發現了！一切終於說得通了！經過二十九年的嘗試和失敗，我終於找到了答案！兒子，我現在已經太老了，無法再做任何事了。你還年輕，你也很勇敢，你有能力能做得到。拯救這個世界，使它免於面臨完全毀滅的命運，是我們的使命。仔細聽著，我無法在這封信中解釋清楚。過來我在樹林中所住的地方，你的姑姑會告訴你方向。趕快過來，我的時間不多了！』」

　　我站起身，打死一隻停在我腿上的蚊子，然後慢慢地走到廚房的流理台，沖洗我的臉和手，試圖回歸現實。

　　「然後……還有後續嗎？」莉亞關切地問著。

　　「沒有了，接著我就起床了，我聽到有人在敲門。是我的哥哥，他問我奶奶生日派對留下的可樂還有沒有剩餘。然後他便開始說起鄰居的保母，還有他坐計程車到超市買好吃的芒果和蘋果派的事。太可惜了……」我回答著。

A short time later, we were visiting Bi Bi's small traditional Taiwanese house with low doorways, next to a decorative temple. Bi Bi was standing on the dark green carpet, looking out of the window and gazing into the far distance. He was preparing himself for the new information that Yen Yen's dreams may have uncovered. He felt touched by our concern and whole-hearted efforts to save the person who wrote the note in the balloon.

"Alright, please tell me what you found out, Yen Yen." Then laughing softly Bi Bi added, "Any headaches, big noses or strange body parts?" Lia smiled broadly. "Sit down on my couch as I clear away some of the stuff and put it in the recycle bin. I don't have a hard-working housewife or a servant to do the housework for me."

I shared the latest news with Bi Bi who tried to relate this dream to the earlier experiences. "But... " Bi Bi said, "there are still too many missing pieces in this puzzle. How is this dream connected to the red balloon?"

"It is plain to see, you must have forgotten something," Lia stated with great confidence. "You must have. Things do not add up. There must have been another dream or maybe part of one is missing and you have to complete it!"

"Possibly," I answered a little confused. "Perhaps I should either play badminton or basketball to see if I can recall something. Will you come along and exercise with me, Lia?"

　　過了不久，我們已經出現在畢畢的傳統台式小屋內，小屋的門口很低，隔壁是一間裝飾華麗的寺廟。畢畢站在深綠色的地毯上，看著窗外，凝視著遠方。他正為顏顏夢境中可能發現的新訊息做好聆聽的準備。對於我們展現出的關心，以及全心全意努力想拯救寫好紙條放進氣球的人，他覺得非常感動。

　　「好了，請告訴我你發現到什麼，顏顏。」畢畢輕輕地笑著，接著說：「有頭痛、鼻子變大，或是身體出現奇怪的部位嗎？」莉亞聽了大笑。「請坐吧，我來收拾沙發上的東西，然後把它們放進回收桶回收。我沒有勤勞的妻子或僕人來幫我做家事。」

　　我告訴畢畢最新發現的消息，他正試著將這個夢和之前經歷到的連結起來。「但是……」畢畢開口說，「這個謎團中還是有太多未解之謎。這個夢與紅色氣球有什麼關聯呢？」

　　「很明顯地，妳一定還忘記了什麼，」莉亞充滿自信地說著。「妳一定還漏了什麼事情沒說，所以整個故事並不完整。一定還有另一個夢，或是妳遺忘了其中一個夢的部分內容，妳必須把它完整地拼湊起來！」

　　「有可能，」我帶著困惑的語氣回答。「也許我應該來打個羽毛球或籃球，看能不能幫助我回想起些事情。妳要跟我一起運動嗎，莉亞？」

Bi Bi's face brightened as he guided us to the basketball hoop in the yard behind his house. " Just the place for you, girls. Have fun. Don't worry about the dog; she doesn't bite. She only barks when she gets excited or sees cockroaches. She also likes to dig holes in the mud. Don't let the ball roll down the hill or it will take at least thirty minutes to get it back!"

Exactly at twelve o'clock noon we came rushing into Bi Bi's house, almost breaking the door down. "There is more!" I yelled with red cheeks from both the excitement and the pleasure of the game. "*In my dream I saw Vincent leaving with a backpack on his back as if he would go hiking or camping. He was wearing a warm sweater plus a winter jacket, a hat, gloves and hiking shoes. Before he walked out the door he hugged his aunt and said, 'Don't worry, this may be dangerous but it must be done. I have to stop the enemy who takes away all meaning in life. It was father's last wish. It is the only way people can continue to exist in this world.' His aunt started crying as she thought he might disappear and never return. Vincent held a red balloon in his hand. Then he wrote on a brown piece of paper with a black writing rock, one of his dad's inventions, and placed it in the balloon. 'If I am not back within one week, please blow up this balloon and hang it on a string out of the window of the apartment building. My father told me there is someone who is able to save me when I am lost. Good-bye, please pray for me!' were Vincent's last words.*"

I closed my eyes, leaned against my chair and asked Bi Bi humbly, "Am I that person?"

當畢畢帶我們到屋子後方庭院中的籃球場時，他的臉容光煥發了起來。「盡情打吧，女孩們。不用擔心那隻狗；牠不會咬人的。牠只有在興奮時，或看到蟑螂時會吠叫。牠也喜歡在泥土裡挖洞。小心別讓球滾下山坡，否則就得花至少三十分鐘才能拿得回來了！」

就在正午十二點時，我們衝進了畢畢家，差點把門都給拆了。「我想起來了！」我大叫著，臉頰因興奮及籃球帶來的激動而染上紅暈。「在夢中，我看見文森背著背包離開，似乎是要去登山健行或露營。他穿著一件溫暖的毛衣，還有一件冬天的夾克、一頂帽子、一雙手套和登山鞋。在他走出門前，他擁抱著他的姑姑，並說：『別擔心，雖然可能會有危險，但是我還是得這樣做。我必須阻止敵人奪走我所有的生存意義。這是父親最後的遺願。這是人類可以繼續存在於這個世界的唯一辦法。』他的姑姑一想到他可能會消失，並且再也回不來時，她哭了起來。文森手中拿著一個紅色氣球。然後他用他父親的其中一項發明——一塊黑色能寫字的岩石，在一張褐色的紙條上寫字，接著將它放入氣球內。『若我一個星期內還沒回來，請吹起這顆氣球，並把它懸掛在公寓的窗外。我的父親告訴我，當我迷失遇難時，有人能夠拯救我。再見，請為我祈禱！』這些是文森最後的幾句話。」

我閉上雙眼，向後靠在椅背上，不確定地問著畢畢：「我就是那個人嗎？」

# The trip of no return?

About three months after my first dreams, Vincent was starting his dangerous trip into the mountains, in an overseas country on the other side of the world. He was thinking back to the last time he had spent with his father.

Mathematics and science had never been Vincent's strong points and he had not finished his secondary education yet. Now, however, the numbers and flowcharts that his dad had showed him were clearly copied and ordered in his memory. It had not been an accident when Vincent had walked into his father's unique brick workshop and Hans had hugged him with tears in his eyes. Vincent had all the skills and logic needed to carry out this very risky job.

"My son," Hans said with a caring voice, "you are the only hope of the populations of all nations. I regret to give you this responsibility, but I don't know anyone else who is both honest and intelligent. You have the skills to successfully complete this mission. Ever since you finished your last term of junior high school I have wanted to spend more time with you, to include you in my life's work. But I was in the middle of testing principles that would support world-changing inventions. I was so close to finding the possible answers. I wanted to fix the horrible events that could lead to the ruin of the earth's social environment and society."

# 回不來的旅程？

　　大約在我第一次夢到文森的三個月後，文森深入世界另一端國家的山區，開始了危險的旅程。他回想起最後一次與父親相處的時光。

　　數學和科學從來不是文森的強項，他也還未完成高中教育的課程。不過現在，那些他父親給他看過的數字和流程圖，都清晰地複製且井然有序地保存在他的記憶中。這一切絕非偶然，早在文森踏入父親那間獨特的磚房工作室，而漢斯含著淚水擁抱著自己的兒子時就已注定。文森已經具備完成這項非常危險的任務所需的所有技巧和邏輯知識。

　　「我的兒子，」漢斯用關愛的口吻說道：「你是全世界人民的唯一希望。我很後悔託付你這樣的重責大任，但是我沒有認識其他既誠實又聰明的人選可以交託這項任務了。你具備能成功完成這項使命的技巧。自從你念完國中的最後一個學期之後，我就一直希望能多花點時間陪伴你，讓你也成為我這一生的成就。但是，我正在試驗能改變這個世界的發明。我就快要找到答案了。我希望能扭轉可能導致地球環境和文明社會毀滅的可怕事件。」

Vincent remembered the precious time spent with his father. He shook his head as if to leave the past behind, and walked with energetic steps up the mountain paths toward his destiny. "Do or die, do or die," he thought to himself as he knew he could not make an error. It might cost him his life. He checked his compass needle and saw it pointing north. "That is the way I need to go to reach my goal!" he said loudly. He wished he could see a golden eagle flying in the sky. His mother had told him when he was young that seeing a golden eagle is always a symbol of success and good outcomes. Then his memories went back to the shocking discovery of his dad.

"Have you ever questioned and debated why there is so much violence and anger in this world? Why people are killing each other and causing so much damage without any real reasons?" Hans had asked him with an unhappy face. "Whole armies are fighting against other armies without ever being told by the presidents of those countries why they are fighting."

"There is a reason for this," his father continued. "The earth is turning faster than before and will keep turning faster in the future. Do you understand what that means? Time is speeding up. There is less time to do everything, so everyone is hurrying and worrying. The pressure of this is influencing the peace and mind-set of the world's population and causing people to attack each other, rather than fixing differences and problems through discussion."

文森想起和父親相處的珍貴時光。他搖搖頭，似乎想從回憶中回到現實，他繼續踩著有力的步伐上山，走向他的命運。「不成功便成仁，不成功便成仁，」他在心裡這麼想著，因為他知道自己不能犯下任何一個錯誤。犯錯可能會使他喪命。他看了看他的指南針，發現它指向北方。「我得朝這個方向前進，達到我的目標！」他大聲地說。他希望能夠看見一隻金色老鷹在天空飛翔。他的母親在他小的時候曾經說過，看見金色老鷹正是成功和好運的象徵。接著，他又想起了父親驚人的發現。

「你是否曾經想過和懷疑過，這個世界為什麼有這麼多暴行和怒火？為什麼人類會在沒有任何理由的情況下互相殘殺，並造成那麼多的傷害？」漢斯面帶憂愁地問他。「各國的軍隊甚至在元首們沒有告訴他們為何而戰的情況下互相攻打對方。」

「這都是有原因的，」他的父親繼續說道。「地球轉動的速度比以往還要快，在未來也會持續以更快的速度轉動。你知道這代表什麼意思嗎？時間正在加速運行。人們可以做事的時間越來越少，所以每個人都處在焦急和擔心之中。這樣的壓力影響了全世界的和平和人類的心態，使人類互相攻擊，而不是透過協議來弭平彼此間的歧異和解決問題。」

Vincent looked at his father hopelessly and said softly, "There must be something that can be done to slow the turning of the earth down. If it keeps going faster and faster human beings will ruin the world."

Hans replied at once, "There is, but there is a price to pay. It will not be easy!" His dad said the words loudly, even though Vincent was standing right next to him.

It seemed nature itself was speaking to Vincent as he was walking up the steep mountain paths, with pockets of snow on both sides, and considered all that his dad had told him. The birds were singing their songs as the wind was blowing through the few trees that could still grow in this cold, but beautiful, mountain scenery. The birds and the trees seemed to beg him to take action, "Go, go, go, time is running out!"

After six hours of hiking the mountain slopes that were becoming harder and harder to climb, his feet were hurting and sore, and his fingers, nose and lips were turning blue due to the cold temperature. He wished he could be bathing in a bathtub with hot water.

Vincent thought to himself, "What in the world am I doing here, am I a loser? I am just at the base of the mountains. I don't know if I can find the waterfalls that flow inside. Will I even be able to survive to tell my aunt about it?" He then purposefully stood up straight and managed to master his fears. He faced the mountains ahead and yelled out loud, "I will obey my father. I will go, continue and succeed. There is no limit to what I can do!" The sound of his voice was repeated softer and softer as it bounced off the mountain sides, until it could be heard no more.

文森沮喪地看著父親，輕聲說道：「一定有辦法可以讓地球轉動的速度慢下來。要是地球持續越轉越快，人類一定會毀滅這個世界。」

漢斯立刻回答：「有的，但是必須付出代價。這不是一件簡單的事！」即使文森就站在父親的旁邊，但漢斯仍大聲地說出這些話。

當文森沿著陡峭的山路向上走，山路的兩邊都積著成堆的小雪堆，他思考著父親對他說過的所有的話，而大自然似乎正在與文森對話。這裡仍有樹木能耐得住這樣的寒冷氣候而繼續生長，當風吹過這些稀疏的耐寒樹木時，鳥兒歌唱著，雖然一片凜寒，但還是構築出美麗的山間風光。鳥兒和樹木似乎乞求著他採取行動，「走吧，走吧，走吧，就快來不及了！」

經過持續六個小時的爬坡山路後，山路越來越難走，文森的雙腳又酸又痛，他的手指、鼻子和嘴唇也因為寒冷而發紫。他希望現在能泡在浴缸的熱水裡。

文森想著：「我究竟在這裡做什麼？我徹底輸了嗎？我還在山腳而已。我不知道我是否能找到隱藏的瀑布。我還能活著回去告訴姑姑這一切嗎？」然後他有意識地站直身體，設法控制他的恐懼。他朝著眼前的山脈吶喊：「我會依循父親的心願。我會繼續前進，然後獲得成功。沒有什麼事是我做不到的！」他的聲音不斷在山中迴盪著，直到聲音越來越小聲，並再也聽不見為止。

# Helicopters or jeeps?

"We will be short of time!" said Lia worriedly. "What is the fastest way to travel to a place that is difficult to get to?"

I was not in the mood to be positive so I answered, "I don't know, even being passengers in an airplane or a fast jeep with four-wheel drive would be totally useless, unless we know where to go. An airplane... an airplane would need a runway, a big area to be able to land, like an airport. I watched quite a few sets of national geographic videos and cable television programs when studying the geography subject in school. There are no airports in mountainous areas!"

"There really are," Lia said, "for example in the Alps, a well-known mountain range in Switzerland, there are small airports so travelers are able to get to the snowfields to ski. I saw photos in magazines."

I realized she was probably right and nodded my head. "But from the airport to the highest mountain we would not be able to use a jeep. Jeeps are not mountain goats! If we need to go to the type of mountain that I saw in my dream, then... then... we would need to use a helicopter and be dropped down holding onto thick ropes!"

Lia shook her head, "A helicopter? Really? That is not going to be cheap!"

"Let's go rollerblading. Or even better, let's go for a jog," she continued. "I just thought of something that could stop us from saving Vincent."

# 直升機或吉普車？

「我們會來不及的！」莉亞擔心地說。「有什麼方法能最快前往難以到達的地方？」

我對這一切也不是很樂觀，所以我回答：「我不知道，就算搭飛機或四輪傳動的吉普車都完全沒用，除非我們知道目的地。一架飛機……飛機需要跑道和能降落的大片空地，就像機場一樣。在學校上地理課時，我看過一些國家地理頻道的影片和電視節目。山區根本不會有機場！」

「真的有機場啦，」莉亞說著，「例如在瑞士著名的阿爾卑斯山上，那裡就有一些小型機場，讓遊客能夠到達山上的滑雪場滑雪。我在雜誌上看過照片。」

我知道她可能是對的，所以我點點頭說：「但是要從機場到達最高的那座山，是無法開吉普車的。吉普車不是高山山羊！如果我們需要前往在我夢裡出現的那座山，那麼……那麼……我們會需要一台直升機，用繩索把我們垂降下去！」

莉亞搖搖頭：「直升機？真的假的？那可不便宜！」

「我們去溜直排輪吧。或者更好的話，去慢跑吧。」她說。「我剛想到一件可能會阻礙我們拯救文森的事情。」

I was quite busy looking in my closet trying to find my jogging pants, and decided not to wear a blouse but the short-sleeved T-shirt that was given to me in senior high school. After I quickly combed my hair something got my attention. The sky looked dark and cloudy. "Of course, the weather! Look on the calendar. It is October, which is in the middle of autumn. It will be Halloween soon, with pumpkin lanterns. But what will the weather be like in that rocky place when we are ready to travel? The climate might be much colder than in Taiwan," I thought.

Lia barely avoided a young boy, who was learning to ride a bicycle on the sidewalk that we were jogging on. Then she said, "Yen Yen, we don't know where to go. It could be in any country that has mountains and waterfalls, and has cold temperatures."

I added, "It also has a red deer."

Unexpectedly lightning flashed from the clouds followed by the sound of thunder. The wind started blowing faster and big rain drops fell down from the sky. Soon small pools of water formed on the ground.

"Lia, did you bring a raincoat? An umbrella will be useless in this wind," I shouted. Lia did not bring anything except for the clothes she was wearing and soon we both looked like cats that had been pulled out of a river.

"Bi Bi's house is nearby," Lia suggested. "Let's go visit him, get dried up and rest, because I also hurt my ankle when I tried to avoid the boy riding his bike."

我忙著翻找衣櫃，想找出我的慢跑褲，然後決定不穿襯衫了，改穿我高中時別人送我的短袖 T 恤。當我快速地梳理完頭髮後，有個東西吸引了我的注意力。天空開始變暗，雲層也越來越厚。「當然，就是天氣！看看月曆。現在是十月，正值秋天中旬。再過不久就是萬聖節了，到時還會有南瓜燈。但是當我們準備前往那個有許多岩石的地方時，會是什麼天氣呢？那裡的氣候一定比台灣冷多了，」我思考著。

我們在慢跑時，莉亞及時閃過一個正在人行道學騎腳踏車的小男孩。接著，她說：「顏顏，我們還不知道目的地。可能是任何有山區和瀑布的國家，而且當地的氣溫一定很低。」

我補充道：「還有一頭紅色的鹿。」

出乎我們的意料，一道閃電劃過天邊，緊隨而來的是一聲驚雷。風開始越吹越急，大顆的雨滴開始紛紛落下。不久，地面就出現許多小水灘。

「莉亞，妳有帶雨衣嗎？現在風很大，沒辦法撐傘的，」我大叫。莉亞除了身上穿的衣服之外，沒有帶其他的東西，很快地，我們就像兩隻剛從河裡爬上岸的落水貓咪。

「畢畢的家就在附近。」莉亞提議。「我們去找他，把身體弄乾，順便休息一下，因為我剛剛在躲開騎車小男孩的時候，不小心扭傷了腳踝。」

"Sit close to my fireplace and warm up," said Bi Bi who had lit a match to start a fire in his fireplace. He was concerned that we would get ill from getting too cold. He tried to ignore that we were dripping water all over the floor and heated up some chicken soup and Beijing duck, which he had made the night before, in the microwave oven. Then he slowly cut an apple in quarters and offered us a piece each.

I was the first one who started talking, "Bi Bi, it is going to be winter in only a couple of months. It will be very cold in the high mountains. Vincent could be trapped, or may not survive without food or shelter. Among the three of us, we need to make progress and find the right place! It will take us at least two or three months to prepare for our trip."

Bi Bi considered telling us everything he had found out. But it seemed wise to omit some things for now. There was one problem that had been bothering him for a long time. "How were two eighteen-year-old girls going to climb high mountains tipped with snow in the middle of winter, possibly in the months of December or January, without any training or survival skills?" He checked his calendar. "How could a young girl take care of herself when hiking mountains? I am an old man, I am seventy years old and I am over-weight," he thought. "I cannot climb steep mountain sides. Maybe they can find Vincent, but how will they get back? Lia and Yen Yen will not be able to take care of themselves, especially if Vincent is weak or wounded."

「坐靠近壁爐取暖吧，」畢畢邊說邊用火柴在壁爐內生火。他擔心我們會因為著涼而感冒。他試著不去注意我們身上不斷滴下、把地板滴得到處都是水的水滴，他還用微波爐熱了一些前一天晚上所做的雞湯和北京烤鴨。然後他慢慢地切開蘋果，給我們一人一塊。

我率先開口：「畢畢，再過幾個月就是冬天了。到時在高山上會非常冷。文森可能會因此被困住，或是因此缺乏食物和遮蔽處，在這樣的情況下，他可能無法存活。我們三個必須想辦法找到正確的地點！我們至少需要兩、三個月來準備這趟旅程。」

畢畢還在考慮是否要告訴我們他發現的所有事情。但是，現在看來似乎有所保留比較明智。另外還有一個問題一直困擾著他。「這兩個十八歲的女孩要如何在寒冷的冬天，可能是十二月或一月的時候，爬上覆滿白雪的高山？她們不僅沒受過任何訓練，也沒習得任何生存技巧。」他看了看月曆。「爬山的時候，年輕的女孩該如何照顧自己呢？我已經是一位七十歲的遲暮老人了，甚至還體重過重，」他想著。「我沒辦法爬上陡峭的山。也許她們能找到文森，但她們該怎麼回來？莉亞和顏顏絕對無法照顧自己的，尤其是如果文森很虛弱或受傷的話。」

Slowly a plan started forming in Bi Bi's mind. He could keep an eye on the small team from the sky, flying overhead as a golden eagle, but he could not be of assistance by helping with practical things. The team needed a coach in charge, someone to teach them how to overcome physical difficulties and how to survive in the mountains, and to protect them.

"But whom, but whom?" Bi Bi lifted his eyebrows until his face looked comical and childish. "No, no, no, not him! He is too crazy, disorganized, foolish... " he stopped in the middle of the sentence. "Perhaps, no... but could it be?" Bi Bi shook his head and rejected the idea. "Stupid idea, I refuse to do that. I must be too tired."

Half an hour later he had decided, he would call Dunkin on his cellphone.

# The coach and other preparations

Bi Bi's thoughts went back to the past when he used to take care of his nephew Dunkin.

He was a skinny little boy with a cap. Dunkin was always very independent from a young age and could usually be found outside playing dodge ball, football and even golf with the local kids. He also liked to watch silly cartoons and seemed to have a marvelous ability to get into trouble and danger with his friends, only to find a way to escape from unusual activities at the last moment.

"My brother and his wife used to call him 'double trouble'," Bi Bi remembered with a smile, "although his classmates envied him for always solving their problems."

慢慢地，一個計畫開始在畢畢心裡成形。他可以化身成金色老鷹，從天空關注她們的安危，但是他無法提供實質上的幫助。她們兩個需要一個教練來教導她們如何克服身體上的困難，在山區存活下來，並保護她們。

「但是該找誰呢？該找誰呢？」畢畢挑起眉毛想著，接著，他的臉上開始出現滑稽和稚氣的表情。「不、不、不，不是他！他太瘋狂、混亂且愚蠢……」他的思緒停了下來。「或許，不……但是，有可能嗎？」畢畢搖搖頭，否定了這個想法。「愚蠢的想法，我才不會做這件事。我一定是太累了。」

半小時後，他決定用手機打電話給鄧肯。

# 教練和其他準備

畢畢的思緒回到了過去，回到他還在照顧他的姪子鄧肯的時候。

鄧肯是一個纖瘦的小男孩，總是喜歡戴著鴨舌帽。鄧肯一直以來都非常獨立，常常都在戶外與當地小孩玩躲避球、足球，甚至是高爾夫球。他也喜歡看愚蠢的卡通，似乎有著和朋友一起製造麻煩和陷入危險的神奇能力，但他總是能在最後一刻找到方法逃離各種不尋常的活動。

「我哥哥和他的妻子過去都叫他『大麻煩』，」畢畢笑著回想，「不過，他的同學們都羨慕他最後總是都能夠順利解決問題。」

Even though Dunkin was often in trouble, Bi Bi had learned to respect him for his goodness, knowledge and wisdom. He could travel in the form of any animal of his choice and change shape instantly. But Dunkin and Bi Bi were not alike. Dunkin had one hidden skill that Bi Bi did not have. In the face of danger he would become as strong as an ox. He would become a protector.

Dunkin was assisting the school coach by explaining the rules of the volleyball game and volleyball net to a group of ninth grade high school students, who were having a PE lesson in their first semester. Over the next couple of months they would also be learning about softball and soccer. They were in the school's large gym, where he was working, when his cellphone rang.

"Practice baseball or volleyball for a while," Dunkin suggested to the twenty-nine students. "Not too noisy please, I cannot hear myself talk!" Bi Bi heard all the background noise and knew there was no way he could explain what was happening over the phone.

"Hey Dunkin," Bi Bi said, "would you like to be a hero?"

Dunkin was instantly interested. "Sure, anytime!"

Then Bi Bi continued, "Come to my house tonight. It is urgent. It is dangerous and it is scary! But the prize you receive, when you are successful, is worth it. We need a hero and a winner."

Dunkin only had time to say okay before he hung up the telephone. "Let's divide into teams and play volleyball!" he yelled above the confusion.

　　雖然鄧肯常常惹麻煩，但由於他的善良、富含學識和智慧，使畢畢對他的尊敬油然而生。他可以化身為任何動物，並能立刻改變外觀。但是，鄧肯和畢畢不一樣。鄧肯還有一項隱藏的技能，是畢畢所沒有的。在面對危險時，鄧肯能變得像牛一樣強壯。他可以變身成一個守護者。

　　在第一學期的體育課堂上，鄧肯正在協助學校教練向一群九年級生解釋排球的比賽規則。在接下來的幾個月，他們還會學習壘球和足球。他們在學校的大體育館上課，鄧肯就在這裡工作，接著，他的手機響起。

　　「大家自己練習棒球或排球一會兒，」鄧肯對這二十九位學生說。「請不要太吵，要不然我會聽不到自己的聲音！」畢畢聽到電話的另一端相當吵雜，知道不可能在電話中把發生的事情一一解釋清楚。

　　「嘿，鄧肯，」畢畢說，「想不想當個英雄？」

　　鄧肯立刻變得興致勃勃。「當然，任何時候都想！」

　　畢畢接著說，「今晚到我家來。非常緊急。此行會有危險，也很可怕！但當你一旦成功之後，得到的獎勵會很值得的。我們需要一位英雄和贏家！」

　　鄧肯在掛上電話前只來得及說聲「好的」。「我們來分組打排球吧！」他在一片混亂聲中大叫。

Dunkin and Bi Bi were sitting comfortably in Bi Bi's small and untidy living room on the old-fashioned sofa that he had cleared in a hurry of all the bundles of notebooks, novels and photos. "You are still as tall and skinny as ever," said Bi Bi with a laugh. "Is it true that you don't like to eat?"

Dunkin replied, "Well, honestly I do not spend much time cooking. I often go to the convenience store or the bakery to buy something to eat when I feel hungry. I like the modern payment system. It is very easy to pay the shopkeeper with my credit card. My favorite foods at the moment are salad, instant noodles, steak, tofu and potato chips from the USA. Once I drove my car to go bowling and I had a flat tire. I also ran out of gas. Then some foreigners came to assist me, one man and one woman. They were speaking English quite formally, calling each other ma'am and sir. The foreigners were friendly and helpful though. They even let me taste some of their salt-and-vinegar potato chips. Ever since then I fancy American potato chips."

After having a conversation for several hours, Dunkin was sitting on the edge of his seat. "When can I go?" he asked eagerly. "I will need to take at least a couple of weeks of vacation to travel all the way to Switzerland."

在畢畢那個又小又凌亂的客廳中，鄧肯和畢畢正舒服地坐在那張舊沙發上，畢畢前一刻才匆忙地整理了沙發上一疊又一疊的筆記本、小說和照片。「你的身材還是跟以前一樣又高又瘦，」畢畢笑著說。「你不喜歡吃東西是真的嗎？」

鄧肯回答：「這個嘛，說實話，我沒有花很多時間在煮飯上。當我餓的時候，通常都直接到便利商店或麵包店買東西吃。我喜歡現代化的付款系統。用信用卡付錢給店主非常方便。我現在最喜歡的食物是沙拉、泡麵、牛排、豆腐和美國的洋芋片。有一次，我開車要去打保齡球的時候，我的車爆胎了。那次剛好也沒油了。然後有兩個一男一女的外國人來幫我渡過這個難關。他們說著相當正式的英語，稱呼對方為女士和先生。他們非常友善且樂意助人。他們甚至讓我嘗嘗他們海鹽口味和油醋口味的洋芋片。從那次之後，我就愛上了美國洋芋片。」

聊了好幾個小時之後，鄧肯正坐在座位的邊緣。「我何時可以出發？」他急切地問。「要去瑞士，我至少需要請假幾個星期。」

As a good host, Bi Bi served Dunkin more French fries and another hamburger and said, "Didn't I see your photo in the newspaper and on TV? I even circled the story with a red marker. News reporters and journalists were talking about a strange happening last year that caused a big traffic jam. I think it was in the spring, maybe in April. A guy jumped off a big waterfall but could not be found and was therefore pronounced dead. It was said that he could have been a thief trying to run away. Many people in the nearby area were interviewed. Some said they saw a black and white wolf or a fox. Others said it could have been a brown bear. For some reason they also showed a picture of you."

Dunkin smiled, "Yeah, I will tell you that story later. I have to go now. I need to go to the barber to get a haircut and dress in my formal suit and necktie. I also need to recharge my phone. Then I will contact my school's principal at her office to ask for either a few weeks leave or for my yearly holiday."

"Training?" said Lia and I at the same time.

"We, Dunkin and I, have a plan to set up an indoor gym with a climbing wall and things to balance and swing on. Even though it is expensive, we feel we need to create an oval running track outside to have a place to run longer distances. Endurance is important when climbing mountains. Remember a thousand mile trip starts with the first step," said Bi Bi.

"Who is Dunkin?" asked Lia, feeling unsure about adding a new person to our group.

作為一個稱職的主人，畢畢給鄧肯更多薯條，並再次端上一個漢堡，他說：「我不是在報紙和電視上看過你的照片嗎？我還用紅色馬克筆把那篇報導圈起來。去年主播和記者都報導著那件造成交通癱瘓的怪事。我記得那起事件是在春天發生的，也許是四月。有一個人從大瀑布上跳下，但卻找不著屍體，因此被宣告死亡。據說他是個小偷，是為了逃跑才這樣做。許多附近的人都接受過訪問。一些人說他們看見一隻黑白相間的狼或是狐狸，其他人則說有可能是一隻棕色的熊。出於某種原因，他們都拍到了一張你的照片。」

鄧肯笑著說：「是啊，我晚點再告訴你那個故事。我得走了。我得先去理髮店剪頭髮，然後換上正式的西裝和領帶。我也需要給手機充電。然後我會在校長辦公室與我任職那間學校的校長碰面，請上幾個禮拜的事假或我個人的年假。」

「訓練？」莉亞和我同時開口。

「我們，也就是鄧肯和我，計畫要架設一間室內體育館，裡面有攀岩牆和一些用於訓練平衡感與擺盪的器材。雖然很貴，但我們覺得還是得在外面設一個橢圓形跑道，讓妳們有地方能練習長跑。登山時，耐力非常重要。記住，千里之行始於足下，」畢畢說著。

「鄧肯是誰？」莉亞問，她對這個隊伍內的新成員感到疑慮。

"Oh, I forgot to introduce Dunkin to you. He is your new coach. Come in Dunkin!" called Bi Bi.

Dunkin had been taking a rest on Bi Bi's bed and sleepily walked into the living room. He stopped and stared at Lia who suddenly felt warm and cozy. They looked into each other's eyes and both became shy.

"Hi, I am Dunkin, Bi Bi's nephew. He asked me to train you to climb mountains and be your coach and hopefully join your team to save Vincent. What do you think?" he finally said. He silently added in his mind, "I would love to be your protector. Wow, that girl is lovely and beautiful. I would like her to be my lady." Then he turned to me and said, "I know all about your dreams and the red balloon. I know how to climb high mountains in winter. I would like to go with you and assist in any way I can."

I answered, "Thanks, I really appreciate that!"

# The mountain hike, animals and a key

Vincent was sitting down on the frozen ground, warming his body by a small burning campfire and holding a bowl of soup in his hands. Then he heard sounds of something, or someone, coming closer. He quickly put down his bowl and moved his hand to the wallet in his backpack to protect the key that his father had given him, when he saw his dad for the last time.

"This key is what I have worked for all my life," Hans had told him with a weak voice. "I have finished my work and I can rest in peace. Now yours has begun."

「噢，我忘了向妳們介紹鄧肯，他是妳們的新教練。進來吧，鄧肯！」畢畢呼喚著。

鄧肯已經在畢畢的床上睡了一會兒，現在睡眼惺忪地走進客廳。他停下腳步盯著莉亞看，莉亞突然感到一股溫暖和舒適感。他們凝視著對方，同時害羞了起來。

「嗨，我是鄧肯，畢畢的姪子。他請我來訓練妳們登山，當妳們的教練，並希望我加入妳們，一起去救文森。妳們覺得如何呢？」他終於開口說道。他在心裡默默補充道：「我非常樂於當妳們的保護者。哇，那個女孩既可愛又美麗。真希望她能當我的女朋友。」接著，他轉向我，對我說：「我已經知道有關於妳的夢的所有事情，還有那顆紅色的氣球。我知道要怎麼在寒冷的冬天登上高山。我希望能跟妳們一起去，並盡我所能地幫助妳們。」

我回答：「謝謝，我真的很感激你！」

# 登山、動物、鑰匙

文森正坐在結冰的地上，依偎著小營火取暖，手裡捧著一碗湯。接著，他聽到了某種物體或人類逐漸靠近的聲音。他立刻放下手中的碗並將手移到背包內的錢包上，保護著裡面的鑰匙，那是他最後一次與父親見面時，父親給他的。

「這把鑰匙是我畢生的努力心血，」漢斯帶著虛弱的聲音告訴文森。「我已經完成了我的工作，可以安詳地離開了。現在，你的工作才正要開始。」

Hans rolled over on his bed and opened his eyes one last time, "A crazy, evil inventor or magician has made a time machine causing the world to turn faster, and has placed it in the mountain with the hidden waterfalls. You need to use the key to change the setting of the machine so it will start slowing the speed at which the earth is turning, until it moves regularly again. Follow the map that I have given you, remember the population of the world is depending on you. Do not let anything stop you!" His father reached out to Vincent to hold his hand and said, "I love you, son."

Hans slowly closed his eyes and entered forever land beyond this physical world.

Vincent heard something and quickly sat up. The noises were getting louder as if a wolf was out hunting alone and had at last found its catch. But the hunted animal made a narrow escape by hiding in a small cave higher up the mountain. After the wolf angrily shook himself from head to toe and disappeared down the mountain, Vincent could see a large male red deer with marvelous horns standing on the mountain side, as if protecting Vincent during the night. Vincent thought he was dreaming and shook his head wildly, "Why is a red deer watching me in the early evening? Perhaps I am not alone."

漢斯在床上翻過身，最後一次睜開眼睛說道：「有一個瘋狂又邪惡的發明家或魔法師製造了一台時光機，讓這個世界轉動得更快，這個人把時光機放在一座有隱藏瀑布的山中。你必須用這把鑰匙去變更機器的設定，讓它開始減緩地球目前的轉速，直到其再一次回到正常的速度。照著我給你的這張地圖走，記住，全世界的人都仰賴著你的行動。不要讓任何事情阻擋你的步伐！」他的父親伸手緊緊握住文森的手，然後說：「我愛你，兒子。」

漢斯慢慢地閉上雙眼，永遠地離開了這個有形的世界。

文森聽到某種物體的聲音，趕緊坐起身子。這個物體逼近的聲音越來越大聲，就好像一匹孤狼在野外覓食，最後發現了眼前的這個獵物。但這隻被獵捕的動物躲在山上較高的一個小洞穴中，最終驚險逃脫孤狼的獵捕。當這匹狼氣憤地甩動全身並從山上消失後，文森看見了一頭大型的紅色公鹿站在山側，牠有著驚人的巨大鹿角，就好像在夜晚負責保護著文森一樣。文森以為自己在做夢，於是用力地搖了搖頭，「為什麼在傍晚會有一頭紅色的鹿看著我？或許我在這裡並不孤單。」

Comforted by that thought, he decided to use his backpack as a pillow and pulled out his sleeping bag. Vincent thought to himself, "I started hiking on Sunday afternoon. Tomorrow it will be Monday. I have to travel at least fifteen kilometers to find the right mountain range." He looked at the map with the chart of the mountain range that his dad had drawn for him, and then checked the positions of the stars. "The deer has put me at ease. I must be going the right way!"

Slowly closing his eyes he sang the poem that his aunt used to sing to him, "Rivers of water, they flow down to the lakes below. Up on the mountains we know the deer are sure to go."

The wolf shook his dark gray fur once more making a bitter, angry sound. Then little by little he turned into a forty-year-old dark-haired man with a square chin, hate in his eyes and crime in his heart. Life had not been good to him. His father used to be a poor factory worker who was always angry. His mother complained from morning till night that she had too many children. When Olec was a child he had known neither love nor care from his parents or brothers and sisters, and he blamed everyone.

He often said, "I have been cheated; life is neither fair nor equal. I do not belong to my home town Omsk, Russia, nor do I belong to my family. I have no faith. Even going to a church and talking to a priest has not given me any comfort. I am as lost as a wave in the center of the ocean, in a never ending storm."

When he was in elementary school he remembered his mother saying, "Olec, we already have enough children. You are one too many!" His father would nod in agreement.

這個想法給文森帶來了安全感，他決定把背包當作枕頭，然後拿出他的睡袋。文森想著：「我從星期日下午開始登山。明天就是星期一了。我必須至少得走十五公里才能到達那個山區。」他看著那張地圖，上面有著山脈分布圖，是父親為他畫的。接著，他看了看星星的位置。「這頭鹿讓我感到安心。我肯定走在正確的道路上！」

他緩緩地閉上了雙眼，哼著之前姑姑經常唱給他聽的那首詩歌：「河流的水啊，向下流往湖泊。上山吧，我們知道那頭鹿肯定會去。」

那匹狼再次地甩了甩身上深灰色的毛，並發出憤怒的嚎叫。接著，牠慢慢地變成一個四十歲的男人，他有著黑髮和方正的下巴，雙眼流露著恨意，內心深處藏著不為人知的犯罪秘密。他的生活一直都過得很艱辛。他的父親之前是一位貧窮的工廠員工，心裡總是帶著憤怒。他的媽媽從早到晚不停地抱怨著自己有太多的小孩要養。當歐列克還小的時候，他從父母或兄弟姊妹身上得不到愛與關懷，於是他把這一切都歸咎到每一個人的身上。

他常常說：「一直以來，我總是受到欺騙；生活既不公平，也不平等。俄國鄂木斯克市不是我的家鄉，我也不屬於我的家庭。我沒有信仰。就算上教堂和牧師談話，也不能帶給我任何慰藉。我就像茫茫大海中迷失的波浪，深陷永無止盡的風暴中。」

當他上小學時，他記得母親說過：「歐列克，我們的小孩太多了。你就是多出來的那一個！」他的父親也點頭表示同意。

"But now I have an aim, a purpose in life. I have an important role to play in the future of the world. I can be smart, terrific and powerful." he clapped his hands to congratulate himself.

"I have invented a time machine that can be employed to make life on earth terrible, and that will ruin all nations. I will trash the world. I will bring poison to the people, like a snake. I will rob them of their peace." Olec laughed angrily while shaking his fist at the sky. "None of the people's lives and families concern me! My knowledge of plants has given me the ability to make a magical mixture so I can turn into a wolf. I will guard the time machine with my life, and I will never quit. No one can save the world ever again!"

"But where should I hide my time machine, my precious robot?" Olec considered the choices. "It is like a chess game; to win the king and queen need to be protected. My main chess piece is the time machine. It needs to be hidden in a place where no one can find it. A spot that is difficult to reach, maybe somewhere in the snowy mountains. It should be a place that I can easily guard and protect as a wolf."

He walked back and forth in his small room, in the basement of an old house, like a caged animal, getting more nervous with every step and then he stood still as if frozen.

"That's it, excellent!" he stamped his feet and yelled so loud that the birds, sitting on the tree outside the bedroom window, flew away in fear.

「但是，我現在有個目標，一個畢生的志願。我將在未來的世界裡扮演著一個重要的角色。我可以成為一個聰明、可怕和掌握權力的人！」他拍拍手鼓勵著自己。

「我已經製造出一台時光機，可以用來給地球上的生命帶來痛苦，這將使所有國家走向毀滅。我將摧毀這個世界。我會像條毒蛇一樣帶給人們毒藥。我會奪走他們擁有的和平。」歐列克憤怒地狂笑著，並對天空揮舞著拳頭。「人類的生命和家人都與我無關！我對植物的認識讓我能夠製造出神奇的藥物，讓我可以變身成為一匹狼。我會用我的生命來捍衛那台時光機，永不放棄。沒有任何人可以拯救得了這個世界！」

「但是，我該把時光機藏在哪裡呢？我那珍貴的機器人。」歐列克思考著可能的藏放地點。「這就像一場西洋棋比賽；需要保護國王和皇后才能獲勝。我最重要的棋子就是這台時光機。它需要被藏在一個沒有任何人可以找得到的地方。一個難以到達的地方，也許是在那個白雪靄靄深山中的某處。這個地方必須是我能以野狼之姿輕鬆守衛與保護的地點。」

他在他的小房間裡來回踱步，他的房間位在一間老舊房子的地下室，這時的他就好像一隻籠中動物，隨著踏出的每一步，他變得越來越緊張，接著，他站得直挺挺地，就像凍結了一般。

「就是那裡，太棒了！」他踏著雙腳大叫，臥室窗外樹上的鳥兒驚恐地飛走。

Then his face became an evil mask, "I heard a speech about wolves being protected in Switzerland. It seems that there are not many wolves left in the Swiss Alps. That would be a good place to hide the time machine, because the person who would try to shoot me with a gun, while I am in the form of a wolf, would be breaking the law and would get into trouble with police officers!"

Olec's face changed to show an evil, sneaky smile as he shouted, "I am on my way. I am better and smarter than everyone else around me. No people can compare with me. They should all be jealous of me. I have the power to overcome the world. I am the judge of the evil actions of men. I will punish them all!"

# Where shall we go?

I thought it would be impossible for me to climb mountains, because I am not as sporty and active as Lia. And I was worried that I might become homesick. So I asked Dunkin, "Do you think I am strong enough to climb high mountains?"

Dunkin looked at me with a big smile on his face, "Of course, Yen Yen, it is Friday, the twenty-third of November. Yesterday we celebrated the Thanksgiving festival. We have been training five hours a day, after school, for almost two months. Both you and Lia have been exercising as if the world is coming to an end. You will be like a mountain goat!" Then Dunkin thought to himself, "Although she is more like a little lamb and I may have to turn into a red deer myself and carry her on my back!"

接著，他的臉變得邪惡，「我聽過一個關於野狼在瑞士受到保護的演講。瑞士的阿爾卑斯山上的狼群似乎不多了。那會是一個隱藏時光機的好地方。因為當我變身成為一匹狼的時候，若有人想要拿槍射我，他就會因此違法，惹上麻煩！」

歐列克大叫時，他的臉上出現了既邪惡又狡猾的笑容，「我要出發了。我比周遭其他人還要強大、還要聰明。沒有人比得上我。他們都應該忌妒我。我有征服世界的力量。我是判官，評判著人類的邪惡行為。我將懲罰所有人！」

# 我們的方向？

我覺得我一定爬不上山，因為我不像莉亞那樣有運動細胞和喜歡活動。我擔心我可能還會想家。所以我問鄧肯：「你認為我夠不夠強壯，能不能爬得上高山？」

鄧肯看著我，給了我一個大大的微笑，「當然，顏顏，今天是十一月二十三日星期五。昨天我們才剛慶祝完感恩節。我們每天放學後都訓練五個小時，已經持續將近兩個月了。妳和莉亞都拼了命練習。妳會像一頭靈敏的山羊的！」接著，鄧肯心裡想著：「雖然她比較像一隻小羔羊，我可能得變成一頭紅色的鹿，背著她前進！」

Dunkin looked at Lia who was wearing jeans and sneakers. She was swinging on a rope in the gym like a female monkey. His heart seemed to grow in size to hold all the happiness he felt, when thinking about sharing an adventure with this special girl. Just in these two months, they had become close friends.

"There is hope for the future, one day I would like to court her," Dunkin said softly to himself. "I will never be bored with her around as my partner. She is my perfect match." Suddenly it became clear to him, "I am developing feelings for her. With her, my life would be complete." Then his cheeks turned red as he saw Bi Bi looking at him curiously.

"Everybody, take a seat somewhere in the living room. Clear away any of my ordinary things, such as diaries and dictionaries," Bi Bi said while looking around his room. There was hardly enough space for Lia, Dunkin, Bi Bi himself and I to sit down. We had just finished eating breakfast together and there was still food on the round table, including half a loaf of sliced bread, jam, a bottle of soda soft drink and a bowl with a large amount of tangerines. It looked like the leftovers of an outdoor picnic. "Oh, I just remembered I also have doughnuts in the refrigerator," Bi Bi added.

He had his hands in the sink and had just turned on the faucet to wash the dishes when he continued, "It is time to make progress and to discuss where we actually need to go to find Vincent." Bi Bi instantly had everyone's full attention.

"But... " I said with surprise in my voice and my heart beating faster. "I thought we didn't know that yet!"

鄧肯看著穿著牛仔褲和運動鞋的莉亞。她正在體育館的繩索間擺盪著，就像一隻靈巧的母猴子。當他想到即將與這位特別的女孩一同冒險，他的內心就雀躍不已，感受到無比的快樂。在這短短的兩個月，他們已經成為了親近的朋友。

「未來總是充滿希望，總有一天我會跟她表白。」鄧肯輕聲地對自己說。「有她在我身邊作為我的另一半，我絕對不會感到無聊。她是完美的伴侶。」突然間，一切都變得清晰，「我對她漸漸產生了感覺。有了她，我的生命才完整。」接著，當他發現畢畢好奇地看著自己時，他的臉頰開始泛紅。

「大家自己清開我的日常物品，像是日記或是字典之類的東西，在客廳找個位子坐吧。」畢畢一邊說一邊環顧客廳四周。這裡幾乎沒有地方能給莉亞、鄧肯、畢畢自己和我坐下。我們才剛吃完早餐，圓形的餐桌上還有食物，有半條切片土司、果醬、一罐汽水和一大碗橘子。看起來就像戶外野餐剩下的食物。「噢，我記得冰箱裡還有些甜甜圈呢。」畢畢補充說著。

他走到水槽邊，伸手擰開水龍頭清洗碗盤，並接著說：「該是有一點進展的時候了，我們要討論一下需要前往何處才能找到文森。」畢畢立刻挑起大家的注意力。

「但是……」我的心臟越跳越快，語帶驚訝地說道：「我以為我們還不知道正確地點呢！」

Bi Bi remembered all his night-time trips flying over the Swiss Alps, and was considering if it would be wise to tell Lia and me everything. "Will they think I am lying or making up a story?" he thought. Finally he said, "Yen Yen, do you remember dreaming about feathers?"

I looked at him strangely, "Of course, but I don't see how that is linked to the place where Vincent may be trapped."

He turned to face everyone, "I saw those same feathers fall when I was flying over the mountains in Switzerland in my dreams. As you know, my grandfather was the village medicine man of this area. He passed on the ability to be a 'dream catcher' and a 'golden skyrider' to me. Therefore I am able to travel the world in the form of a golden eagle during my sleeping hours." Bi Bi looked at Dunkin with a concerned look on his face.

Dunkin nodded and said to us, "I am one of Bi Bi's relatives. I know this is a fact."

Bi Bi continued, "Yen Yen, we have seen the same feathers, but I did not just see the feathers. I saw them falling on the top of a mountain. When I flew close to that mountain I heard the sound of waterfalls rushing down. But I couldn't see the waterfalls, only an exit. There was a man-made tunnel on the south side of the mountain. I believe that Vincent may have gotten trapped in an underpass, inside the tunnels where the waterfalls flow."

I could not believe my ears. "That sounds too easy. The answer to the problem is almost too good to be true," I thought to myself. "But why would there be feathers falling on top of the mountain where Vincent might be? What do the feathers mean?" I questioned Bi Bi. Now it was Dunkin's turn to look at Bi Bi to see if he agreed.

畢畢想起自己每夜飛到瑞士阿爾卑斯山的情景，猶豫著現在該不該把一切都告訴我和莉亞。「她們會不會認為我在說謊，或是編造故事呢？」他思考著。最後他終於說：「顏顏，妳還記不記得你夢見了羽毛？」

我奇怪地看著他，「當然，但是我不知道這與文森被困在哪裡有什麼關聯。」

他轉身面向大家說：「當我在夢中飛到瑞士阿爾卑斯山上時，我也看見了相同的羽毛落下場景。你們都知道，我的祖父從前是這個地區村莊的藥師。他把『捕夢人』及『幻金天騎』的能力傳給了我。所以，我在睡覺時，能以金色老鷹之姿遨遊世界。」畢畢臉色凝重地看著鄧肯。

鄧肯點頭，並向我們說：「我是畢畢的親戚。我知道這是真的。」

畢畢繼續說著：「顏顏，我們都看見相同的羽毛了，但是我不只看見羽毛，我還看見它們落在一座山頂上。當我飛近那座山時，我聽見了瀑布沖刷而下的水流聲。但是我沒看見瀑布，我只看見一個出口。在那座山的南面有一條人造隧道。我相信文森應該被困在底下，也就是瀑布所在的隧道內。」

我簡直不敢相信我的耳朵。「那聽起來太簡單了。這個問題的答案簡單到不可置信。」我自己想著。「但是，為什麼文森所在的那座山會落下羽毛呢？那些羽毛又代表什麼意義呢？」我問畢畢。現在，輪到鄧肯看著畢畢，等著畢畢同意。

Bi Bi said, "Go ahead, Dunkin, it is the perfect time for them to know!"

Dunkin walked to the bedroom and pulled out one of the drawers in Bi Bi's dresser. In the back of the drawer under a pile of magazines, carefully hidden to stop anyone from stealing it, there was a package. It was a dark purple book wrapped in an old cotton cloth. He very carefully put the book on the dining table.

"This book," Dunkin said with a respectful voice, "is a treasure. It has been in our family for a long time. It was generously given to us by a man who came to visit Taiwan at least sixty years ago. This man introduced himself by the name Alfred. He said he lived with his family in a wooden house called a Swiss chalet, on one of Switzerland's highest mountains, close to the city Bern. Alfred said he did not just travel to Taiwan as a visitor to learn about Taiwan's culture and history by finding books in bookstores and libraries. He was looking for the grandson of the well-known village medicine man who, as someone told him, lived on a hill near Hualien. Then Alfred said, 'I need to deliver this book. Do you know where this person lives?' "

Bi Bi smiled and added, "I was only ten years old when he knocked on our door! I was so excited that a visitor from far away Switzerland was looking for me. 'I am Bi Bi,' I stated proudly. 'I am the grandson of the village medicine man!' " Lia was so curious to find out what was written in the book, that she pushed Dunkin out of the way and insisted on opening the book that instant.

I interrupted Bi Bi and said, "But... what does it say about feathers in the book?"

畢畢說：「去吧，鄧肯，現在是時候讓她們知道一些事情了！」

鄧肯走向臥室，拉開畢畢衣櫥內的其中一個抽屜。抽屜深處有著一疊雜誌，藏在雜誌底下的是一個小包裹，它被刻意藏起來避免被人偷走。它外面包著舊棉布，裡面是一本深紫色的書。他非常小心地將書放在餐桌上。

「這本書，」鄧肯用著崇敬的語氣說著：「是一個寶藏。它在我們家已經傳承了很久。這本書是一位六十年前造訪台灣的人所贈予的。這個人向我們介紹自己的名字是艾爾弗雷德。他說他與家人住在瑞士山區其中一座山峰中的一間木屋裡，稱之為瑞士小木屋，靠近伯恩市。艾爾弗雷德表示，他並非一個來台灣旅遊、只想從書店和圖書館的書本內學習台灣文化和歷史的觀光客。他正在尋找村裡知名藥師的孫子，有人告訴他，這位藥師的孫子住在靠近花蓮的小山丘上。艾爾弗雷德說：『我需要把這本書給他。你們知道這個人的確切住址嗎？』」

畢畢笑著補充：「當他來敲門時，我才十歲！我非常興奮有人遠從瑞士前來找我。『我叫畢畢，』我驕傲地向他介紹自己。『我是村裡藥師的孫子！』」莉亞非常好奇地想知道書上到底寫了些什麼，她擠開了鄧肯，堅持立刻打開書來看看。

我打斷畢畢，說著：「但是……書中寫了關於羽毛的哪些事呢？」

Bi Bi shook his head, "Patience, patience, girls. Behave yourselves, don't be impolite. I will explain about the feathers very soon. The history and life story of our mysterious guest, named Alfred, will be told later."

# The ancient book

A soft light seemed to shine from the book, as if it was asking to be opened. Bi Bi stepped forward to open the book, since it was personally given to him when he was ten years old. But as soon as he touched the book he became dizzy and had to let go of the cover.

"What?" Bi Bi was worried. "What happened? I opened it before, about eight months ago. I think it was the beginning of March. Why will it not allow me to open it now?"

I softly touched Bi Bi on the arm and felt a little embarrassed, "The book... the book is speaking to me in my mind! It is asking me to open it, why?"

Bi Bi calmed down and answered, "Of course, why didn't I think of that? Yen Yen has been called in her dreams to save Vincent. The book knows her."

Dunkin looked puzzled, "What is that smell? When Yen Yen touched the book it smelled like roses and pineapples. Did you see the thin fog around the book? It looked like white smoke slowly going up into the air. It almost seemed like the book was saying thank you!"

畢畢搖搖頭，「耐心點、耐心點，女孩們。克制自己，不得失禮。我很快就會開始解釋羽毛的事了。晚點會跟妳們說我那位神秘訪客艾爾弗雷德的過去及故事。」

# 那本古書

書中似乎散發出一道柔和的光線，就好像自己要求被打開一樣。由於這本書在畢畢十歲時就被書的主人親自交到他的手中，因此畢畢很自然地走向前準備翻開那本書。但是當他一碰到書的時候，便開始感到頭暈目眩，畢畢只好放開手。

「怎麼回事？」畢畢很擔心。「發生什麼事了？我之前打開過它，大約在八個月前。我想是三月初的時候。現在為什麼不讓我打開它？」

我輕輕地用手臂推推畢畢，有點不好意思地說：「這本書……這本書正在跟我的內心對話！它要我打開它，為什麼？」

畢畢冷靜了下來並回答：「噢，當然，我為什麼沒想到呢？顏顏在夢中被呼喚前往拯救文森。這本書認識她。」

鄧肯臉上出現了困惑的表情，「那是什麼味道？顏顏一碰到那本書時，它便散發出玫瑰和鳳梨的香味。妳看到這本書周圍那層薄薄的霧了嗎？看起來像是白煙慢慢飄向空中。就像是這本書正在道謝！」

The magical book opened easily when I lifted the cover. Rather than using Chinese characters or English alphabet letters in a text, the book was telling a story by means of drawings and paintings, like a comic book. The story described future events that had not happened yet. It showed a young man trapped in an underground tunnel.

"That is Vincent, he looks like a prince!" both Lia and I shouted.

"Fantastic," said Lia. "I wonder if Vincent really looks like that."

While everyone had their full attention on the book, Bi Bi saw something falling out of the book and softly landing on the floor. It was a white envelope. But not only that, several small black spiders also fell out of the book and ran under the sofa. He quickly picked up the envelope and put it in his pocket. "I will have a close look at it later," he decided. "This may affect future events after this mystery is solved."

On the next page it showed hundreds of colorful birds painfully pulling out their feathers and letting them fall on the top of a mountain. In the distance a young man could be seen playing magical music on a flute.

Bi Bi's eyes were bright, "I know this story, the birds agreed to assist, and answered the call of the magical flute. They did not mind feeling pain if it would save the world from ruin. The feathers were signs to guide the team looking for Vincent."

當我翻開封面時，這本神奇的書輕易就被打開了。內容不是用中國文字或英文字母寫成的，而是以素描和圖畫來說故事，就像一本漫畫書。故事敘述著還沒發生的未來事件。上面顯示著一個年輕人被困在地底的隧道中。

「那是文森，他看起來就像一位王子！」我和莉亞異口同聲地說道。

「太奇妙了，」莉亞說著。「我想知道文森是不是真的長得就像那個樣子。」

當每個人的注意力都放在這本書上時，畢畢看見有東西從書中掉了出來，輕緩地落在地板上。那是一個白色信封。但是不僅如此，還有幾隻黑色的小蜘蛛也一起掉了出來，然後牠們跑進沙發底下。他迅速地撿起那個信封，並把它放進口袋裡。「我晚點再仔細看看，」他決定後說道。「在這個謎團解決後，這也許會影響未來發生的事件。」

在下一頁，內容說著幾百隻五彩繽紛的鳥痛苦地拔下自己的羽毛，讓它們從山頂落下。在遠處，可以看見一位年輕人用長笛吹奏著神奇的音樂。

畢畢的雙眼發亮，「我知道這個故事，鳥兒同意幫忙，並回應著神奇長笛的呼喚。如果能夠拯救這個世界不致毀滅，牠們不會在意痛苦。這些羽毛是指引我們尋找文森的關鍵。」

When I turned the page everyone looked shocked. The picture showed a greedy angry wolf with large pointed teeth chasing a large red deer with big horns. Bi Bi put his hand on my arm and said softly, "This is a warning. There will be dangers and troubles. You may have problems. It seems like someone tried to stop Vincent and will also try to stop you. In my latest dreams I kept seeing a machine that was sending out an electrical current that made the world turn faster, and a metal key that fits into a triangular lock. If someone made these, then I think..."

Bi Bi was interrupted by Dunkin who could not stay silent any longer, "Excuse me, Bi Bi, do you think the wolf is protecting the machine?"

"Possibly," answered Bi Bi who didn't want to share everything he was thinking until he had considered all the possibilities. "Let's first have a good night's sleep. Remember, joy comes in the morning! Warm milk is served for everyone!"

I did not sleep that evening till midnight. My alarm clock, which was given to me for my birthday by my younger cousin, fell on the floor with a big bang, when my shoulder hit it by accident. Suddenly a thought entered my mind, "If there is a link between Vincent and me. If I am called to save him, and our story was written in the distant past. I am not sure but... maybe I should be able to talk to him in my dreams!"

I got out of bed and walked in my pajamas to the bathroom to get the small bottle with green dreaming juice off the wall shelf above the bathtub. "Where is it? Don't tell me I lost it! Oh, it was hiding behind my toothbrush and my bottle of liquid soap that is shaped like a cute bear."

當我再翻開下一頁時，每個人都嚇到了。圖畫中顯示著一匹貪婪憤怒的野狼，這匹有著尖牙利齒的野狼追著一頭有著大角的巨大紅鹿。畢畢把手放在我的手臂上，輕輕地說：「這是一個警示。顯示接下來會出現危險和麻煩。你們可能會遇到問題。看起來是有人想要阻止文森，也會試圖阻止你們。在我最近的夢境中，我一直看見有一台機器不斷地發送出電流，使地球轉動得更快，還有一把能插入三角形鎖頭的金屬鑰匙。如果有人製造這些，那麼我認為……」

畢畢的話被鄧肯打斷，鄧肯再也無法保持沉默，「不好意思，畢畢，你認為那匹狼是在保護那台機器嗎？」

「可能是的，」畢畢回答，在思考過所有可能性之前，他不想說出他所想的一切。「我們今晚先來睡個好覺。記住，喜悅會在早晨來臨！每個人都可以享用溫熱的牛奶！」

那天晚上直到過了半夜以後，我才入睡。我的鬧鐘是我的表妹送給我的生日禮物，當我的肩膀不小心碰到它時，它掉到地上發出了巨大的聲響。突然間，我的腦海中出現了一個想法。「如果文森和我之間存在著某種連結。如果我是受到呼喚要去拯救他，而且我們的故事在遙遠的過去就已經被寫下。我不確定，但是……也許我能夠在夢中跟文森交談！」

我爬下床，身上還穿著睡衣，走進浴室，打算拿出浴缸上方牆上架子上的那瓶小瓶綠色引夢藥。「它在哪裡？不要告訴我我把它弄丟了！噢，它躲在我的牙刷和有著可愛小熊瓶身的沐浴乳後面。」

I felt both rushed and excited so I quickly swallowed more of the ancient herbal mixture than I had planned to. I did not want to be too stingy and not drink enough. When I had stopped drinking I looked at the bottle and got scared. "Oh no, I was half asleep and drank almost one-third of the bottle, what will happen to me? Well, there is nothing I can do about it now." I jumped back in my bed and fell asleep within eleven minutes.

# A conversation in the night

I focused with all my might on Vincent and what he could be doing in the dark tunnels under the mountain. I imagined what he would look like, using the picture of him in the magical book as a guide. With Vincent on my mind, and the dark green herbal drink moving through my body, I was soon in a deep sleep.

Bi Bi suddenly jumped out of bed. "Something is totally wrong, very wrong!" he shouted, even though there was no one in his little house to hear him. His body was shaking and his heart was beating so fast that Bi Bi was worried he would have a heart attack. It took him at least ten minutes to calm down, but he still felt very uncomfortable. "It must be Yen Yen," he finally thought. "She has made a mistake, but what? I need to know how to cure her!"

我又急又興奮，所以一下子就吞下好幾口古藥草汁，比我原先計畫要喝的分量還要多。我不想因為捨不得喝而喝得不夠。當我停下時，看著瓶身，我嚇了一大跳。「噢，不，我在半夢半醒間喝了幾乎三分之一的量，接下來我會發生什麼事呢？好吧，現在我也無能為力了。」我跳回床上，在十一分鐘內就睡著了。

# 夜晚的對話

我專注地想著文森，並想著他在山下的黑暗隧道中可能正在做什麼。我靠著魔法書中的照片想像著他的樣貌。不斷地想著文森，加上深綠色的藥草汁在身體中流竄，我立刻陷入熟睡。

畢畢突然跳下床。「有一件事情完全錯了，錯得離譜！」他大叫著，雖然小屋中沒有人。他的身體開始顫抖，他的心臟跳得非常快，畢畢甚至擔心自己心臟病要發作了。他花了至少十分鐘才冷靜下來，但是他仍然感到非常地不安。「一定是顏顏，」他最後終於想到了。「她犯了一個錯誤，但是，是什麼呢？我必須找到治療她的方法！」

*In my dream I was flying over lands and oceans without knowing where I was going. After what seemed like forever, I landed in a strange place. I was in a place where I had never been before. "Where am I? I am so afraid and alone," I said quietly. Then softly in the distance I heard a soft voice calling me.*

*"Are you coming to save me? Did you see the red balloon?" I lifted my head and looked around me to find out who was talking. "Answer me, answer me please!" The voice became even softer until I could not hear it anymore.*

*I yelled, "Vincent, Vincent, is that you?" But there was no reply.*

*Twenty minutes later I thought I heard the same voice saying, "Yes, yes, I am. I am waiting for you!"*

*Then there was only silence except for some sounds I had never heard before. I seemed to be in a desert with no mountains at all, only a couple of trees and a few small areas of grass could be seen here and there. To my surprise I saw a big male kangaroo under a tree watching me from a distance. In one of the other trees I saw a koala eating some leaves while carrying a baby koala on its back.*

*Drums were beaten louder and louder, followed by the appearance of a group of native Australians wearing strange clothes and war paint on their faces and bodies. They yelled at me, "What are you doing here? This is the land of our Gods. This meeting is men's business, no women are allowed! You should know this! Go away now!"*

I started tossing and turning in my bed. *"I have to run away,"* I thought, *"but my legs do not seem to be able to move."* The loud ringing of my cellphone woke me up at five in the morning.

在夢中，我飛過大片的陸地和海洋，不知道自己該往哪裡走。經過了一段看似永遠的時間之後，我降落在一個奇怪的地方。我身在一個以前從未到過的地方。「我在哪裡？我感到既害怕又孤單。」我輕聲地說。接著，我聽見了遠方有人小聲地呼喚我的聲音。

「妳是來救我的嗎？妳有沒有看見那顆紅色的氣球？」我抬起頭看看四周，想找出是誰在說話。「回答我，請回答我！」這個聲音變得越來越微弱，直到我再也聽不到。

我大喊：「文森，文森，是你嗎？」但是沒有任何回應。

二十分鐘後，我想我又聽到了同樣的聲音說著：「是的，是我，我在等妳！」

接著，除了一些我從未聽過的聲音外，四周只剩一片寂靜。我似乎身處於一片沙漠之中，附近沒有任何一座山存在，放眼所及只有幾棵樹和些許的小塊綠地。出乎我意料之外的是，我看見遠方樹下有一隻大型的公袋鼠，正盯著我看。在其中一棵樹上，我看見一隻無尾熊正在嚼食葉子，背上還背著一隻無尾熊寶寶。

背景的鼓聲越來越大聲，接著出現一群澳洲土著，穿著奇怪的衣服，臉上和身體上畫著出征的圖騰。他們朝我吶喊：「妳在這裡做什麼？這裡是我們的神明之地。這場會議是男人的事，女人不能參加！妳應該知道才對！現在離開！」

我開始在床上翻來覆去。「我必須離開，」我想著，「但是我的雙腿似乎無法動彈。」我的手機在清晨五點響起，把我叫醒。

"Yen Yen, are you alright?" Bi Bi waited nervously for me to answer.

"Oh, Bi Bi, I am so glad you called me. That was terrible, what a bad dream. I couldn't run away!" I was rubbing my eyes and carefully felt my head. Then I said, "Bi Bi, I have a very big headache."

Bi Bi answered, "drink some water and try to get some rest. I will ask Lia to go visit you later."

At eight o'clock in the morning Lia came to see me. "Did you speak to Vincent? How do you know it was him?" She asked while sitting on a yellow chair with metal legs next to my bed, holding an ice-pack on my forehead. I pushed her hand away.

"Lia, that is way too cold, please get me some medicine for my headache," I complained.

"Well, I am not a driver of a car yet, but maybe I can ride my bicycle to the drugstore," Lia answered.

"Oh, that is too much trouble. I think I have painkillers in my handbag." I sat up in my bed a little too fast and slowly lay back down. Then I thought maybe putting some cream on my face would make me feel better, so I pulled a tube of face cream out of my bag also.

"Lia, it seems I can talk to him in my dreams, but because I took too much dreaming juice I went all the way to the island continent of Australia. I could not hear him very well. The contact was very weak. He talked about the red balloon. Lia, it was really him!" Lia jumped out of her chair and almost pushed me out of bed by giving me a big hug.

"Ouch," I shouted, "remember the headache!"

「顏顏，妳還好嗎？」畢畢緊張地等著我回答。

「噢，畢畢，我真高興你打電話來。剛才真是太糟了，我做了一個噩夢。我在夢中無法動彈！」我揉揉雙眼，認真地感覺我的頭是否還好。接著，我說：「畢畢，我的頭好痛。」

畢畢答道：「喝點水然後休息一下，我會叫莉亞待會過去找妳。」

莉亞在早上八點鐘的時候來找我。「妳跟文森說話了嗎？妳怎麼會知道那是他呢？」她坐在我床邊一張有著金屬椅腳的黃色椅子上問道，她正幫我扶著額頭上的冰敷包。我推開她的手。

「莉亞，太冰了，請給我一些頭痛藥，」我抱怨著。

「這個嘛，我還不會開車，不過也許我可以騎腳踏車去藥局幫妳買，」莉亞回答。

「噢，那太麻煩了。我想我的手提包裡有一些止痛藥。」我從床上坐起身，但是起身太快讓我的頭更痛了，所以又慢慢地躺下。然後我想，在臉上擦些乳液應該會讓我感覺好些，所以我再從包包裡拿出一條乳液。

「莉亞，我似乎能在夢中跟他對話，但是因為我喝了太多引夢藥，所以我一路到達澳洲的小島上。我聽不太清楚他的聲音。我們之間的連結非常微弱。他有提到那個紅色的氣球。莉亞，真的是他！」莉亞從椅子上跳起，給了我一個大大的擁抱，她的力道大得差點把我推下了床。

「哎呀，」我叫著，「我的頭還痛著呢！」

Lia ignored my complaints and said cheerfully, "Do you get it? You can talk to Vincent! You can ask him what he needs and where he is! Oh, Yen Yen, the possibilities are endless."

Some time later, Vincent, trapped in the Swiss high mountains, was madly trying to find new ways to get out of the big hole in the frozen ground that he had fallen into. He stopped for a second and considered how one unguarded moment could change everything. Of course there had been a very good reason to be in a hurry. A dark gray wolf had been following him. At first he had not noticed, but then he had seen a small movement on the snow out of the corner of his eye, as if an animal was hunting him or was quietly trying to get closer.

"I don't understand," Vincent thought to himself. "Why would a wolf be interested in me? Oh, no! I could be his afternoon snack." Vincent almost started laughing. "I am sure I don't taste yummy." He climbed out of the big hole and started walking faster. Suddenly he was very frightened when he realized he would not be able to outrun this wild wolf. "I don't have a gun, only a short hunting knife. In a fight the wolf would surely win."

Hundreds of thoughts started racing through his mind as he brushed his wavy brown hair out of his eyes. "The wolf is linked to the time machine!" Suddenly there was no doubt in Vincent's mind. "I must be close to its hiding place." Then there was only darkness as he fell in another larger hole that was the entrance of a medium sized cave. "Ouch," he yelled as he felt a sharp pain in his head.

莉亞忽略我的抱怨，興高采烈地說著：「妳知道嗎？妳可以跟文森交談！妳可以問他需要什麼幫助，還有他在哪裡！噢，顏顏，這大有可為啊。」

不久後，困在瑞士高山上的文森，由於不小心掉入了結冰地面上的一個大洞裡，正瘋狂地尋找能從洞裡脫身的各種方法。他停了一會兒，思考著若有這麼一刻能卸下防備心，是否會發生什麼改變。當然，現在是應該要著急才是。有一匹深灰色的野狼正跟著他。一開始，他沒有注意到，但在某個瞬間他的眼角餘光看見了雪地上有個東西移動了一下，看起來像是有一隻動物正在追捕著他，或正在伺機接近。

「我不明白，」文森想著。「為什麼這匹狼會對我感興趣？噢，不！我有可能會成為牠的下午茶點心。」文森幾乎笑了出來。「我確定我一點都不美味。」他從那個大洞裡爬了出來，並且越走越快。突然間，他感到驚恐，因為他知道自己可能會被這匹野狼追上。「我身上沒有槍，只有一把短獵刀。若我跟牠打起來，野狼一定會贏的。」

他一邊撥開眼前波浪狀的褐色頭髮，心裡也開始湧現千百種思緒。「這匹狼一定跟時光機有關！」那一瞬間，文森非常肯定這一點。「我一定非常接近時光機的藏放之處了。」接著，他失足跌入另一個更大的洞，眼前只剩一片漆黑，那個洞是一個中型洞穴的入口。「好痛！」他大叫著，頭部感到一陣劇痛。

# We are on our way

"We will have to leave soon," thought Dunkin as he was cutting some branches off the big tree growing next to his driveway, in front of his house. Though he realized that climbing a ladder with a heavy metal saw should have all his attention, he could not keep his mind on the job. He had the insistent feeling that we needed to go soon. "The weather is getting much colder. It is December now and in the middle of the winter season. In January it will be close to the end of the winter, and there will surely be too much snow to climb the high mountains in Switzerland. Today's date is Tuesday, the tenth of December. I am glad Bi Bi arranged airline tickets for us and advised us to set off next week Thursday."

Dunkin smiled as he remembered Lia jumping up and down with the airplane tickets in her hand.

"We got them, we got them. Hip, hip, hooray, we are on our way!" Lia became so excited that she ran to Dunkin and gave him a big hug and said, "This will be the adventure of our lifetime. Nothing can stop us now!" Bi Bi and I were both sitting on the couch and couldn't help laughing at Dunkin as he looked shocked.

Dunkin said quietly to himself, "I am the luckiest person in the world. Traveling and saving the world, together with Lia, will be both wonderful and scary." That instant he felt his ladder shaking. "Oops, I'd better climb down quickly, there is no way I can go on this trip with a broken leg. That would be a major problem." He climbed down the ladder and picked up his big iron hammer, which he had left on the ground and started cleaning up the driveway.

# 開始出發

　　「我們必須儘早出發，」鄧肯內心想著，一邊動手鋸斷他家門前車道旁那棵大樹的樹枝。雖然他知道拿著一把沉重的金屬鋸子攀爬梯子時必須專注小心，但是現在他還是難以專心。他知道我們必須盡快出發。「天氣變得越來越冷。現在已經是十二月了，冬季已經過了一半，等到隔年一月便是冬末了，瑞士高山上的雪一定會多到無法上山。今天是十二月十日星期二。我很高興畢畢幫我們處理好機票了，並且建議我們下週四出發。」

　　鄧肯想起莉亞拿著機票，興奮地跳上跳下的樣子，臉上露出了笑容。

　　「有機票了，有機票了。耶，耶，萬歲，我們要出發了！」莉亞興奮極了，她跑向鄧肯，給了他一個大大的擁抱，說著：「這會是我們今生最令人難忘的冒險。沒有什麼事情可以阻止我們的腳步！」我和畢畢坐在沙發上看著鄧肯驚訝的模樣，忍不住笑了出來。

　　鄧肯在心裡想著：「我是全世界最幸運的人了。能和莉亞一起遠行和拯救世界，將會是件令人害怕卻又格外美好的事情。」在那一刻，他發覺腳下的梯子在搖晃。「噢，我最好快點下去，要是腿受傷了，肯定沒辦法參與這趟冒險之旅。這會是個大問題。」他爬下梯子並拿起之前放在地上的大鐵鎚，開始著手清理車道。

On Sunday, the fifteenth of December I was going for an early morning walk. I dressed in my running uniform and added a thick winter coat plus a colorful scarf. "I need some time to be alone. I feel like I have forgotten to do something important. But what is it? Walking in the forest outside of Hualien may help me remember things," I said, while shaking my head to clear my mind.

"It is only a couple of days before we fly to Switzerland. We have airplane tickets for Thursday, the nineteenth of December at seven o'clock in the morning. That will only be a couple of days before Christmas. During that time there will be many festivals, but the preparations for our trip are more important. We have everything to climb mountains and, hopefully, survive. Our parents have agreed to let us go on an educational trip to travel around the mountains of Switzerland under the watchful eyes of Dunkin and his wise uncle Bi Bi. Our backpacks are filled with tents, cooking pots and other camping tools. Our clothes are warm enough to survive in minus zero weather. But... " I kicked a branch off the footpath while talking to myself, "I cannot get Vincent out of my mind."

I sat down on a low wooden bench by the side of a stream, and felt inspired by the nature I saw around me. On my left side I could see a beautiful spot with green plants covering the lower hills and some parrots flying from tree to tree. The mountains seemed to stand as giant guards protecting the local area. Far in the distance I saw several hunting birds with large wings flying high in the sky.

　　十二月十五日星期日，我正準備要去早晨健走。我穿上運動服，外面搭上一件厚厚的冬天大衣，再配上一條五彩繽紛的圍巾。「我需要一些獨處的時間。我覺得好像有一件重要的事情我忘記去做了。但是，是什麼事呢？在花蓮外的森林裡散步也許能讓我想起一些事情，」我說著，一邊搖頭清理思緒。

　　「再過幾天，我們就要飛到瑞士了。飛機起飛的時間是十二月十九日星期四，早上七點鐘。距離聖誕節只剩幾天而已。那時一定會有許多慶祝活動，但是出發前的準備顯然更重要。我們已經準備好爬山需要的每個裝備，希望我們能安然渡過。我們的父母也同意我們在鄧肯和他那充滿智慧的叔叔（也就是畢畢）的把關下，踏上這一趟富有教育意味的瑞士高山之行。我們的背包裝滿了東西，有帳篷、鍋子和其他露營工具。我們也帶了足以保暖的衣服，讓我們能夠渡過零下低溫。但是……」我一面把腳邊的一根樹枝踢離小徑，一面自言自語：「我一直無法忘記文森。」

　　我坐在小溪邊的一張低矮木椅上，感受到身邊自然美景的激勵鼓舞。在我的左側，我可以看見低矮的山丘上長滿了綠色的植物，還有幾隻鸚鵡在樹間來回飛行。這些山看起來就像巨大的士兵，守衛著這個地區。在遠處，我看見幾隻正在獵食的老鷹，牠們正張開巨大的雙翅在天空高飛翱翔。

"I wonder if Bi Bi is that kind of eagle in his dreams. I guess so," I thought quietly. "There is peace and inclusion in nature, all animals and plants live together in agreement and freedom. It would be terrible if all this beauty would disappear." I started listening to the sounds around me. I could hear the rushing sound of the water going down the stream and the small croaks of the little frogs as they seemed to tell each other their daily news.

Some gray monkeys could be seen busily eating the fruit of some nearby trees and bees were buzzing in pretty purple flowers. "This is a beautiful quiet place, maybe I could... Even if Vincent was talking softly..." I talked seriously to myself, "Yen Yen, you are daydreaming! You do not have special magical gifts like Bi Bi. Your parents are normal people. Most likely the only reason Vincent talked to me in my dream was because I took too much of the dreaming juice." But the thought was unshakable and kept bothering me. "Maybe I should give it a try?"

I focused with all my heart and mind on Vincent, as I had seen him in the ancient purple book. I tried to imagine how he would feel when being trapped and trying to survive. Then I said kindly, "Vincent, Vincent, can you hear me?" I paid attention for several minutes and said it louder, "Vincent, I believe you can hear me! Stop what you are doing and listen carefully!" Instantly it seemed all animals and plants hushed their sounds. To my surprise there was total silence. I felt like I was in a circle of quiet. It could be compared to a message channel.

Then, uncertainly, a voice could be heard. "Who are you?" it said softly as if it had come from a long distance. I almost fell off the wooden bench that I was sitting on, not sure if I was excited or scared.

「我想畢畢在夢中是否就是化身成那種老鷹。我想是吧，」我靜靜地想著。「大自然中有種寧靜和包容性，所有的動物和植物都在協議下共生共存，並享有自由。這樣的自然之美若是消失了，那就太可怕了。」我開始聆聽周圍的自然聲音。我聽得見溪流中湍急的水流聲，小青蛙此起彼落的呱呱聲，牠們似乎在互相傾訴今天遇到的新鮮事。

我看見一些灰色的猴子忙碌地享受著附近枝頭上的果實，蜜蜂在美麗的紫色花叢間嗡嗡地鳴叫。「這裡真是一個既美麗又寧靜的地方，或許我能……就算文森說話的聲音很輕……」我嚴肅地對自己說，「顏顏，妳正在做白日夢！妳不像畢畢有特殊的神奇力量。妳的父母只是一般人而已。文森在夢中會跟我說話的原因很有可能只是因為我喝了太多的引夢藥。」但是這個想法似乎沒有因此退散，反而不斷地出現。「或許我該試試？」

由於我曾經在紫色古書中見過他的樣子，所以我開始全神貫注地想著文森。我試著想像他被困住、努力求生的感覺。接著，我親切地說：「文森，文森，你聽得到我說話嗎？」我仔細傾聽了數分鐘後，開始更大聲地說：「文森，我相信你聽得到我說話！現在停下你手邊的事，仔細聽我說！」突然間，所有的動物和植物似乎都開始噤聲。出乎我意料之外，周圍變得一片寧靜。我覺得我好像身處在寂靜無聲的世界中。現在的情形好比進入一個通訊頻道。

接著，隱隱約約中，我聽見了一個聲音。「妳是誰？」這個聲音很輕，彷彿是從很遠的地方傳來的。我差點從木椅上摔下來，不確定我現在的心情是興奮還是害怕。

"Vincent, I had dreams of a red balloon. Not just one dream but many. A piece of old brown paper fell out. There was a note written on it asking for help, did you write that?" It took at least five minutes to receive an answer as if the person speaking was deciding if I could be trusted.

"Yes, that was me, Vincent. You must be the person that my father said would help me if I was in trouble. What is your name?" he replied.

"I am Yen Yen, I live in Taiwan," I said shyly.

Vincent said, "Taiwan, I have no idea where that is. Oh, isn't that an island somewhere close to Japan?"

# The trap and the plan

Olec, in the shape of a wolf, walked angrily in circles around the big hole in the ground about sixty-four kilometers from the city Bern in Switzerland. He said hatefully, "I could have easily attacked him and killed him. He seemed to be alone! Why would a boy climb mountains in this empty frozen area? It is impossible to find fresh food here. He seems too young to be by himself. What does he have to gain by being here? Is he just a careless teenager who wants to show off how sporty and strong he is by doing something dangerous and risky?" Olec pointed his wolf ears and shook his body from head to tail. As wolves' senses are very strong, hearing being one of the strongest, he was able to hear sounds from up to sixteen kilometers away in an open area.

　　「文森，我夢到了一個紅色的氣球。它不只一次在夢裡出現，它在我的夢中出現了很多次。一張舊舊的褐色紙條從裡面掉出來。上面寫著求救的訊息，是你寫的嗎？」至少過了五分鐘後，我才聽到回應，似乎說話的這個人正猶豫著，不知道該不該信任我。

　　「是的，那就是我，文森。妳一定就是那位我父親曾經提過，當我遇險時，會前來幫助我的人。妳叫什麼名字？」他回答著。

　　「我是顏顏，我住在台灣，」我害羞地說著。

　　文森說：「台灣，我不知道那在哪裡。噢，是不是靠近日本的一座小島？」

# 陷阱與計畫

　　變成狼的歐列克憤怒地繞著地上的大洞踱步，此地距離瑞士伯恩市足足有六十四公里之遠。牠憤恨地說：「我原本可以輕易地攻擊他，然後把他殺掉的。他看起來只有一個人而已！為什麼在這樣結凍的荒地中會出現一個男孩？這裡根本不會有新鮮的食物。他看起來年紀很小，根本不可能獨自一人生活。他來這裡到底有什麼目的？還是他只是個魯莽的青少年，為了炫耀自己的運動能力和證明自己強壯的體魄，才做這麼危險和冒險的事嗎？」歐列克伸直了狼耳朵，從頭到腳抖動了一下牠的身體。由於狼隻擁有敏銳的感官，而聽力更是其中強項，因此牠能在空曠的地區中，聽到十六公里外的聲音。

"I hear a human voice! He may be wounded but he is still alive! But... who is he talking to? Maybe he is one of those crazy people who talks to himself. Is it possible that he may know about the time machine? Does he have a purpose for being here?" The wolf bitterly looked at the moon that gave the snow a strange blue glow, as if it was the scenery of another planet.

"I cannot guard him here forever, in thirteen minutes I will change back into an ugly man. I will freeze and die of hunger if I stay here."

Then Olec laughed with an evil look in his eyes, "It will be fine, perfect! I don't have to kill him. He will not survive because he cannot climb out of the hole. There is no food and no water down there, not even insects to swallow. Nobody can save him now!" Olec, in the form of a wolf, ran home at his top speed of nearly sixty kilometers an hour. "This is better than having a car. I am a genius!" he said with a false, sneaky smile. "If others would know about my secret herbal drink, they would all be envious of me. Nothing can stop my evil plan!"

Bi Bi was talking to Dunkin on the phone as he sat in the small noodle shop that sold the well-known Taiwanese black bean noodles. He ate at this noodle shop often and had gotten to know the owners and customers in the shop over the many years that he had lived in the local area. "Dunkin," he said into his cellphone, "I need some advice. Do you have a minute to talk?"

"Sure," came Dunkin's cheerful voice loud and clear.

"I am worried about Vincent. If he is trapped somewhere in the Swiss Alps then how will he eat? By the time he is found, he may have died of hunger. The food in his backpack will have disappeared into his stomach long ago," said Bi Bi.

「我聽到人類的聲音！他可能受傷了，但是他還活著！可是……他在跟誰說話呢？或許他跟其他人一樣瘋了，正在自言自語。他有沒有可能知道時光機的事呢？他來這裡究竟有什麼目的？」這匹狼憤恨地凝視著月亮，月光使得雪地反射出奇怪的藍光，不真實地就像是在另一個星球上的景色。

「我無法永遠守在這裡防範他，再過十三分鐘，我就要變回一個醜陋的人類了。如果我再繼續待在這裡，我會因為飢寒交迫而死去。」

接著，歐列克帶著邪惡的眼神笑著，「沒關係，太好了！就算我不殺他。他也絕對活不了的，因為他根本無法從那個洞裡脫困。下面沒有任何食物，也沒有水，甚至連可以生吞的蟲子都沒有。現在沒有人能夠救得了他了！」變成狼的歐列克用接近時速六十公里的最快速度飛奔回家。「這比擁有一台車子還棒。我真是個天才！」他一邊說著，一邊露出虛假、狡猾的笑容。「要是有人知道我的神奇藥水的秘密，他們一定都會忌妒我。沒有人能夠阻止我的邪惡計畫！」

畢畢正坐在一間小麵店跟鄧肯通電話，這家麵店賣著台灣有名的黑豆麵。這麼多年來他都住在這一區，也常常在這家麵店用餐，所以認識麵店老闆和這裡的熟客。「鄧肯，」他對著電話說，「我需要一些建議。你現在有時間說話嗎？」

「當然，」鄧肯歡喜的聲音既宏亮又清楚。

「我擔心文森。如果他被困在瑞士阿爾卑斯山的某處，那他要如何吃東西？等我們找到他時，他可能早就餓死了。他背包內的食物可能撐不了那麼久，」畢畢說著。

Dunkin was silent and unsure what to say, "Hmm... there could be a method to get basic needs like food and water to him, but I have never tried it before. It can only be done if we know his correct position, I guess."

Bi Bi ate some more noodles, drank his dumpling soup and had a sour orange for dessert. Still with his mouth full, he answered, "To find out where he is at the moment you may need to search that part of the mountain range. We know the general area around the mountain with the waterfalls. Both of us have been there. We cannot waste anymore time."

Dunkin put a plan together in his mind. "Yeah, I think I can do that. The weekend is starting tomorrow. I will drink some warm milk and go to bed early tonight."

Bi Bi nodded happily, as if Dunkin could see him on video rather than having a discussion on the phone. "OK, let me know what happened on Monday!"

Dunkin fell into a deep sleep as soon as his head touched his pillow. The clouds were moving fast across the sky and seemed to be playing a hide-and-seek game with the moon. The wind was blowing continually from the west. Dunkin knew what was going to happen. He had made these night-time trips many times before. In an instant his body started shaking and changing into a mighty male red deer with big horns. From head to feet he measured about a hundred and eighty centimeters.

　　鄧肯沉默了，不確定該說些什麼，「嗯……可能有一個方法可以滿足他基本的需求，像水和食物，但是我之前從來沒有嘗試過。我想，只有在知道他的確切位置之後，才有可能做得到。」

　　畢畢繼續吃著麵，喝著餛飩湯，並吃一些酸橘子當作點心。雖然嘴巴裡塞滿了食物，但他仍開口答道：「為了找到文森目前的位置，你可能需要搜尋那個部分的山區。我們知道有著瀑布的那座山的位置。我們兩個都去過那裡。不能再浪費時間了。」

　　鄧肯在心裡制訂了一個計畫。「是啊，我想我可以做到。明天就是週末了。我今晚會喝些溫熱的牛奶，然後早一點上床睡覺。」

　　畢畢開心地點頭，像是鄧肯可以從視訊看見他，而不是只在電話中進行討論。「好的，星期一讓我知道事情的後續！」

　　鄧肯一躺在枕頭上，就立刻睡著了。雲層在天空中快速地移動著，就好像在和月亮玩捉迷藏一樣。空中不斷地吹送著西風。鄧肯知道接下來會發生的事。他之前在夜間就已經走過這趟路線好幾次了。突然間，他的身體開始顫抖，然後變身成一隻頭上有著大角的巨大紅色公鹿。從頭到腳，牠大約有一百八十公分高。

His four legs stood confidently on the white snow of the freezing cold mountains in Switzerland. "This must be the one," he thought as he pointed his ears and moved them in the direction of the sound. "I can hear the water rushing down the hidden waterfalls. But how can I get to the waterfalls?" With his sharp eyes the deer could see clearly in the dark. Soon he had spotted a man-made tunnel that seemed to lead under the mountain. The big red deer stopped and smelled the air around him, "Should I go inside?" He shook his head wildly, showing his big neck muscles. "No, Vincent is not there." He suddenly felt with total certainty that Vincent was somewhere else. Perhaps he was only a short distance away.

Then when the wind changed and started blowing from the east, he heard a weak voice softly calling, "Help me, help me!" As the deer went towards the sound, he realized that it was coming from a deep hole in the ground, so deep that he could not see the bottom.

Dunkin moved through space, and turned back into a twenty-year-old sports coach in his bedroom in Taiwan. "We don't have much time. I cannot get him out of the hole. I need to talk to Bi Bi this instant!" Dunkin jumped out of bed, got his coat and put it on while walking to the front door. "I have to tell Bi Bi now; it doesn't matter what time it is!"

　　牠的四隻腳穩健地踩在瑞士山上的雪地上。「一定是這座山沒錯了，」當牠把耳朵朝著聲音的來源豎起時，牠這樣想著。「我可以聽到水流從隱藏瀑布沖刷而下的聲音。但是，我該如何進入那個瀑布呢？」這頭鹿有著銳利的雙眼，能夠在黑暗中看清事物。不久，牠就發現了一個人造的隧道，似乎深深打入這座山。這頭紅色巨鹿停下來嗅了嗅周圍的空氣，「我該進去嗎？」牠用力地甩了甩頭，顯現出牠強壯的頸部肌肉紋理。「不，文森不在那裡。」突然間，牠很確定文森在其他的地方。或許是離這裡不遠的地方。

　　接著，當風向改變，開始吹起東風的時候，牠聽到了一陣微弱的聲音，呼喚著：「救我，救我！」當這頭鹿開始朝著聲音的來源前進後，牠發現聲音是從一個通往地底深處的洞口中傳來的，那個洞非常深，深到牠完全看不見洞底。

　　鄧肯開始穿越空間，變回一個二十歲的運動教練，回到台灣的臥室中。「我們的時間不多了。我沒辦法從洞裡救出他。我必須立刻跟畢畢說！」鄧肯跳下床，抓起外套，一邊走向門口，一邊穿上外套。「我必須現在就告訴畢畢；我才不管現在幾點了！」

# Food and water

First the doorbell was ringing, and then there was a loud knocking on the door of Bi Bi's little house on the hill. "Who needs to visit me in the middle of the night?" Bi Bi turned over in his bed and thought he was dreaming, but then sleepily rolled out of bed to open the front door when the knocking continued. "Dunkin, what are you doing here?" he called out.

"Sorry to wake you. Please excuse me," Dunkin answered as he almost pushed past Bi Bi into the living room. "Oh, Bi Bi, we are out of time. I found Vincent. But... we have to do something this instant. Now, now, we have to do it now!"

Bi Bi walked to the sink to pour himself a glass of water. "Dunkin, slow down, what are you talking about? Please sit on a chair and tell me what happened."

Dunkin was silent for a second and tried to control his emotions. "Vincent has had an accident. He has fallen into a deep hole. I don't think he has reached the time machine yet. Oh, Bi Bi, I think he has been there awhile. His voice sounded very weak. We need to find a way to give him his basic needs, such as food and water, as soon as possible!"

After Bi Bi went to the restroom to go to the toilet and washed his face and hands, he boiled some water and poured it into his teapot. "Let's have a cup of tea together. It is a victory that you found Vincent. Finally we know where he is! Good news to tell the girls! But now we have to feed him. If he does not make it to the time machine then the population of this world and the earth's environment will have lost all hope of survival. There will be no future at all."

# 食物和水

先是門鈴響起，接著，畢畢位於山上的家傳出大力的敲門聲。「是誰非得在三更半夜來找我？」畢畢在床上翻了翻身，以為自己是在做夢，但當敲門聲繼續時，他睡眼惺忪地從床上起身，打開前門。「鄧肯，你在這裡做什麼？」他喊著。

「抱歉吵醒了你。請原諒我，」鄧肯一邊回答著，一邊與畢畢擠身而過走向客廳。「噢，畢畢，我們快沒時間了。我找到文森了。但是……我們必須趕緊有所作為。現在，就是現在，我們必須快點行動！」

畢畢走到水槽邊，給自己倒杯水喝。「鄧肯，慢點，你在說什麼？請坐，然後告訴我發生了什麼事。」

鄧肯安靜了一會兒，試著控制自己的情緒。「文森發生意外了。他掉進一個很深的洞裡。我覺得他還沒有找到時光機。噢，畢畢，我想他已經在洞裡待一陣子了。他的聲音聽起來很虛弱。我們得想辦法給他補充基本的必需品，像水和食物，且越快越好！」

畢畢走進浴室上廁所，並沖洗了臉和手後，他煮了些開水，把它倒進他的茶壺中。「我們先喝杯茶吧。你找到了文森，這是一大進展。至少我們知道他在哪裡了！有好消息可以讓女孩們知道了！但是現在，我們必須給他食物。如果他無法找到時光機，那麼全世界的人，還有整個地球環境將會失去生存的希望。世界將毫無未來可言。」

Bi Bi seemed absent-minded as he made a list in his mind of how to get prepared for this sudden trip abroad.

Dunkin sat at the dining table eating pizza, hot dogs, corn and an apple. "Bi Bi, I always need a lot of energy after midnight adventures. I apologize for getting fresh food from your refrigerator and freezer."

Bi Bi smiled at his younger nephew, "No problem. Go for it. Help yourself." Then his face brightened, "Of course the book... the magical purple book that Alfred brought. I remember the next page. Wasn't there a picture of a golden eagle carrying a bag in its claws and flying over the snowy mountains?"

Dunkin stopped eating and looked excitedly at Bi Bi, then he replied, "Right, excellent. We are both thinking the same thing. That may be the best method!"

Bi Bi said goodbye to Dunkin and pushed a button in the kitchen to start his hot water pump. "I'd better have a hot shower and get ready to go!"

Forty minutes later, at five o'clock in the morning, Bi Bi was flying over lands and seas, over China and part of Europe until he arrived in Switzerland. He loved flying over the ever changing scenery. "This is true freedom," he thought to himself as he felt the motion of his great wings as a golden eagle. "I would not trade this feeling for anything. On the land I feel like an elephant, heavy and slow. Up here, high above the ground, I feel like the king and the wide blue sky is my kingdom."

　　當畢畢在心裡列出要如何準備這一趟突如其來的國外旅程的清單時，顯得相當心不在焉。

　　鄧肯坐在餐桌邊吃著披薩、熱狗、玉米和蘋果。「畢畢，在深夜冒險旅途後，我總是需要補充大量的能量。我從你的冰箱和冷凍庫中拿出新鮮的食物，我為此道歉。」

　　畢畢對著他的年輕姪子笑著，「沒問題。吃吧。一切自己動手！」接著，他的臉亮了起來，「當然還有那本書……那本艾爾弗雷德帶來的紫色魔法書。我記得下一頁的內容。不是有一張圖片畫著一隻金色老鷹，用爪子鉤著一個袋子，飛往白雪皚皚的山上嗎？」

　　正在吃東西的鄧肯停了下來，興奮地看著畢畢，接著，他回答：「沒錯，好極了。我們想的是一樣的。這可能是最好的辦法！」

　　畢畢對鄧肯說聲再見後，按下廚房的一個按鈕，啟動熱水馬達。「我最好先洗個熱水澡，然後就可以準備出發了！」

　　四十分鐘後，就在凌晨五點鐘，畢畢飛過陸地和海洋，飛越中國和部分歐洲，到達了瑞士。他喜歡飛過千變萬化的風景。「這才是真正的自由，」牠一邊想著，一邊感受著身上巨翅的擺動：「我絕對不會把這種感受拿去換任何東西。在陸地上，我覺得自己像隻大象，既笨重又緩慢。在這裡，高高的天上，我就好像是個國王，而這片廣闊的藍天就是我的王國。」

In his big claws he was carrying a bag with food and water for Vincent. Bi Bi was concerned that he would not make it in time. "Will the boy be dead?" he thought nervously. "Will I be too late? If Vincent cannot reach the time machine, will the world be ruined just because of a lack of food?" With his sharp eagle eyes he was studying the mountain side, searching for the hole that Vincent had fallen into. Dunkin had made a map for him on the computer, but now he had to depend on his senses to find him. The golden eagle swept down and then he saw it! Just as Dunkin had described it!

He heard a soft begging sound, "Someone help... someone help..."

Bi Bi quickly dropped the bag into the hole and hurried home as storm clouds were gathering in the distance.

# Exams and links

Because Lia and I are classmates, we had been studying vocabulary words together in our classroom to prepare for our final exams, while listening to popular pop music on our cellphones. I said, "We'd better focus, we only have a short time to study before we go to Switzerland. Our tests are in March and we need to have good scores. That is only a couple of months away."

"Let's first go for lunch in the school cafeteria, my stomach is starting to make funny noises," Lia laughed, while putting away her artwork, homework and other textbooks, and clearing the desks.

牠的巨爪鉤著一袋要給文森的食物和水。畢畢擔心自己沒能及時趕到。「這個男孩會不會因為撐不下去而死掉？」牠不安地想著。「我會不會來不及？如果文森無法找到時光機，這個世界是否會因食物來不及送達而被毀滅？」牠用那雙銳利的鷹眼掃視山側，尋找文森跌入的那個洞穴。雖然鄧肯用電腦幫牠繪製了一張地圖，但是現在，牠必須倚賴自己的直覺來找到文森。這隻金色老鷹環顧底下，然後終於發現了這個洞穴！就跟鄧肯描述的一樣！

牠聽到了一個虛弱的乞求聲，「來救……來救我……」

畢畢迅速地將那袋食物丟進洞穴中，然後趕緊飛回家，因為不遠之處開始聚集了層層的暴風雲。

# 考試與心靈連結

因為我和莉亞是同班同學，為了準備期末考，我們一起待在教室裡，一邊聽著手機播放的流行音樂，一邊讀完了單字。我說：「我們最好專心一點，距離出發去瑞士之前，我們能夠讀書的時間不多了。我們三月就要考試了，而且必須要拿到好成績才行。距離考試只剩下幾個月而已了。」

「我們先在學校餐廳吃午餐吧，我的肚子已經餓到咕嚕咕嚕叫了，」莉亞笑著說，她收拾好她的作品、回家作業和其他課本，並把桌子整理乾淨。

I nodded and said, "I'd better take all our notes off the blackboard, clean it and collect the chalk and the glue, before the bell rings again to start a new class. We don't want the teacher to get angry with us for not being tidy."

In the cafeteria we ordered spaghetti, buns with black bean paste, and a fruit salad with peaches and pears as a side dish. We liked to eat at the school cafeteria as the fee was quite cheap. During our meal we discussed the preparations for our travel abroad.

Suddenly I started feeling very uncomfortable and dizzy. "Lia," I said, "I think I am sick. Hmm... perhaps not sick but feeling very strange. Can you bring me home? No, no, not home. I don't need to lie down. Oh, I know. We need to go see Bi Bi. It has something to do with Vincent!"

Soon we were stepping out of Bi Bi's second floor living room onto the small balcony, which was like a platform reaching over his backyard. From his house on the hill we could see his garden, with a goose and a hen looking for small seeds in the grass, and a small pond with a couple of turtles dreaming on the rocks. Further in the distance the beautiful scenery of the river and the mountains touched our hearts. It seemed as if an artist had painted the scene and had added extra color.

Bi Bi pulled out some chairs and brought us some glasses with soft drink. "Sit down, Yen Yen. We may have to nurse you back to health. Do you have a fever or the flu? You are looking pale. Do you need to see a doctor or should I call an ambulance?" Bi Bi looked at me closely.

我點點頭，說道：「我最好在下一節課打鐘之前，把黑板上的筆記全部擦掉、清理乾淨，並收好粉筆和膠水。最好不要因為沒整理好東西而讓老師生氣。」

在自助餐廳裡，我們點了義大利麵、黑豆糊小圓麵包，以及水蜜桃與梨子的水果沙拉當作配菜。我們喜歡在學校裡的自助餐廳裡用餐，因為費用相當便宜。我們在用餐期間討論著出國旅行前的準備工作。

突然間，我開始感到非常地不舒服和頭暈。「莉亞，」我開口，「我覺得我生病了。嗯……也可能不是生病，就是一種很奇怪的感覺。妳可以帶我回家嗎？不、不，不是回家，我還不需要躺下。噢，我知道了，我們得去見畢畢。這和文森有關！」

很快地，我們就通過畢畢家二樓的客廳走到外面的小陽台上，這個小陽台像是一個連接後院的平台。畢畢的家位在一個山丘上，我們可以從這裡看到他的花園，花園中有一隻鵝和一隻母雞正在草地中尋找小樹籽來吃，裡面還有一個小池塘，旁邊的石頭上有幾隻烏龜正做著白日夢。再遠一些，河流和山脈的美麗景色觸動著我們的心靈。一切看起來就像一個藝術家畫出來的美景，甚至還添上美麗的顏色。

畢畢拉出幾張椅子，為我們倒了幾杯汽水。「請坐，顏顏。我們也許得讓妳恢復健康。妳有發燒或流感的症狀嗎？妳的臉色看起來很蒼白。妳需不需要看醫生？或是需要叫救護車嗎？」畢畢仔細地打量著我。

"I do not have a stomachache. My stomach just feels very empty," I answered. "It feels like I have not eaten for many days. But that does not make sense at all. I just ate a big lunch together with Lia. Bi Bi, I really don't understand. This is scary."

"Oh, I understand." Lia dropped herself down on the sofa. "How could I be so stupid? It all makes sense. Bi Bi just told us what happened to Vincent. Don't you get it? Vincent is hungry and his stomach is empty. He feels dizzy and weak. Yen Yen, you are feeling the same. There seems to be a special link between you and Vincent." Lia continued, "Did you talk to Vincent today?" I shook my head.

Bi Bi stopped sweeping and mopping the floor and said, "I dropped a bag of food into the hole last night, but Vincent may not have seen it. The food and water are there, but I assume he may have been too weak to notice it. Yen Yen, you have to tell him before it is too late!"

I walked up the hill behind Bi Bi's house, where he stored all his buckets, damaged furniture and garbage bins. "The only way I can talk to Vincent is by finding a quiet place in nature," I thought to myself. "I need to focus." I sat down on a big round rock facing the tops of the trees growing in the valley below. In my mind's eye I could see Vincent lying down on the dirty ground of the cave. A couple of meters away from him there was a bag with food and water. "Vincent, Vincent," I started calling him. "Vincent, this is Yen Yen. Look around you, there is a bag with food and water next to you. Eat and drink!" No answer, silence seemed to continue forever.

Then finally I heard a voice that was quiet and weak. It was, without doubt, Vincent's voice. "Yen Yen, I found the bag. Thank you, thank you. I don't understand. There must have been an angel caring for me!"

「我的肚子不痛。我只是覺得我的肚子非常空，」我回答著。「感覺就像是我已經好多天沒吃東西了。但是這根本說不通。我中午才跟莉亞一起吃了一頓豐盛的午餐。畢畢，我真的不知道為什麼。我好害怕。」

「噢，我懂了。」莉亞噗通一聲猛然坐上沙發。「我怎麼會這麼笨？這一切都說得通了。畢畢才跟我們說過文森的事而已。妳瞭解了嗎？文森現在非常餓，他的肚子是空的。他也會感到頭暈和虛弱。顏顏，妳現在和他有著相同的感受。妳和文森之間似乎有著一種特殊的連結。」莉亞繼續說，「妳今天有跟文森說過話嗎？」我搖搖頭。

畢畢停下掃地和拖地的動作，說著：「我昨晚丟下一袋食物到洞裡，但是文森可能還沒有看到。水和食物已經在那裡了，但是我想他也許過於虛弱了，所以沒有發現那袋東西。顏顏，妳必須在一切太遲之前，告訴他這件事。」

我走上畢畢家後方的小山丘，那裡存放著畢畢所有的桶子、損壞的家具和垃圾桶。「我唯一能跟文森說話的方法就是在大自然裡找一個安靜的地方，」我想著。「我需要專注。」我在一塊大圓石上坐下，面對著從底下山谷中長出的樹頂。我可以從心裡看見文森平躺在骯髒的洞穴地上。離他幾公尺遠的地方就是那個裝滿食物和水的袋子。「文森、文森，」我開始呼喚他。「文森，我是顏顏，看看你的四周，你旁邊有一袋食物和水。趕快吃點東西喝點水！」沒有傳來任何回應，這樣的寂靜似乎永無止盡地延續著。

接著，我終於聽到一個非常小聲且虛弱的聲音。毫無疑問地，那是文森的聲音。「顏顏，我找到那個袋子了。謝謝妳，謝謝妳。我不明白，但一定是有一個天使在守護著我！」

I answered, "I am so glad you found the bag. Eat a little at the time. I cannot do anything else to cure any wounds you may have, but stay strong and have courage. We are coming." I softly started to sing a song to comfort him, "I see the sun coming over the mountains, chasing the darkness away. It is a new world, a new life. It is a new world that will never die. All of our fears washed away."

Then all I heard was, "Thank you, thank you." The sounds slowly became softer and were soon gone.

Vincent could hardly believe it. First a girl called Yen Yen started speaking to him and then a bag with food appeared in the hole, which was really the entrance of a medium-sized cave. "She keeps talking to me, fantastic. I have heard her voice not just twice, but three times now!" He smiled because he knew how crazy that sounded. He was surprised that they were able to talk to each other over such a long distance and said softly, "She must be an angel, or someone with magical powers. I don't have any other explanation. I wonder if I will ever meet her." Then he thought, "Why does she even care about me?"

"But it's not the right time to think about the girl. There must be a way to get to the time machine, I cannot waste anymore time!" Vincent felt his heart beating faster as the pressure of the responsibility of saving the world, which he was carrying on his shoulders, was becoming heavier. "I have to find a way out!" He slowly tried standing up and cried out in pain. He carefully touched his head and neck and realized they were bleeding. He tried to wipe them with a handkerchief, but soon found out he could not get the bleeding to stop.

　　我回答：「我很高興你找到那個袋子了。別一口氣吃太多。雖然我無法治好你身上的傷，但是你必須保持健康和勇氣。我們要準備出發了。」我開始輕輕地唱起歌來安撫他，「我看見太陽從山上升起，驅離黑暗。這是一個新世界，一個新生活。這是一個永不止息的新世界。我們所有的恐懼都被驅散了。」

　　接著，我聽到的都是：「謝謝妳，謝謝妳。」這個聲音逐漸變小聲，不久便消失了。

　　文森幾乎不敢相信。首先，有個名為顏顏的女孩主動跟他說話，接著，一袋食物就出現在洞裡，這個洞正是這個中型洞穴的入口。「她竟然能持續跟我對話，太神奇了。我聽到她的聲音不只兩次了，現在是第三次！」他笑了，因為他知道這聽起來有多瘋狂。他非常地驚訝他們能橫跨那麼遠的距離對話。他輕聲地說著：「她一定是一個天使，或者是有著神奇力量的人。我沒有辦法想到其他的解釋了。我想知道的是，自己是否有機會能夠見得到她。」接著，他想到：「為什麼她會在乎我呢？」

　　「現在不是想那個女孩的時候。一定有辦法能找到時光機，我不能再浪費時間了。」當文森感受到所肩負的拯救世界的責任越來越重時，他的心跳越來越快。「我必須找到出去的方法！」他慢慢地嘗試著起身，然後因為身體的痛苦而忍不住大叫。他小心地摸了摸自己的頭和脖子，才發現它們正在流血。他試著用手帕擦拭血跡，但不久就發現無法止血。

"I will have to tear up one of my shirts to make a long piece of cloth to put around my head and neck," Vincent said loudly to give himself courage. He found that he could not move his neck, and tried to keep it as still as possible while walking to the back of the dark cave. Suddenly he heard the sound of hundreds of black wings moving above his head. He quickly hid behind a rock. "What was that?"

# Bats, tunnels and airplanes

Vincent turned on his flashlight and was surprised to see hundreds of bats flying near the ceiling of the cave. Even more bats were hanging upside down holding onto rocks and old tree roots. "I must have woken them up. Too late now, I hope they will not see me as an enemy and attack me. I seem to remember my biology teacher said that most bats only eat insects, so I will just ignore them."

The ceiling of the cave was becoming lower and after two hundred meters the cave had changed to a narrow tunnel. Vincent had to go down on his hands and knees to go forwards. He was getting worried when he realized that it would be impossible to turn back. "What will I do if this is a dead-end tunnel? No one will be able to find me down here, I will be trapped. How can I be so dumb to do this?" Vincent stopped himself by saying aloud, "Stop it, this is the only chance to get out. It is not possible to climb out of the deep hole. This is my only hope!" He started coughing because of the polluted air in the tunnel but kept going forward.

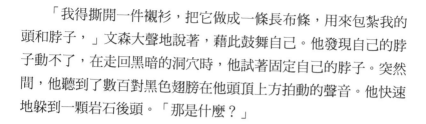

「我得撕開一件襯衫，把它做成一條長布條，用來包紮我的頭和脖子，」文森大聲地說著，藉此鼓舞自己。他發現自己的脖子動不了，在走回黑暗的洞穴時，他試著固定自己的脖子。突然間，他聽到了數百對黑色翅膀在他頭頂上方拍動的聲音。他快速地躲到一顆岩石後頭。「那是什麼？」

# 蝙蝠、洞穴和飛機

文森打開手電筒，很驚訝地發現有數百隻蝙蝠在洞穴上方的洞壁盤旋著。還有更多蝙蝠倒吊在岩石和老樹根上。「我一定是把牠們吵醒了。現在才意識到這件事已經太晚了，我只希望牠們不會把我當作敵人，然後攻擊我。我依稀記得生物老師曾經說過，大部分的蝙蝠只吃昆蟲，所以，我只要不理會牠們就好了。」

越往洞穴內前進，洞穴變得越來越矮，走了約兩百公尺後，洞穴開始變成一條狹窄的隧道。文森不得不跪下，以雙手扶地的姿勢向前爬行，才能繼續前進。當他發現不可能回頭的時候，他開始感到憂心。「如果這條隧道的盡頭是條死路，我該怎麼辦？沒有人會發現我在這裡，我會被困住。我怎麼會這麼笨，做出這種蠢事？」文森藉由大聲叫喊來阻止自己的胡思亂想：「停下來，這是唯一能出去的希望。要爬出這麼深的洞是不可能的。這是我唯一的希望！」由於隧道內的空氣相當汙濁，他開始咳嗽，但是他依舊繼續向前邁進。

After going on his hands and knees for two and a half hours, his pants had been torn at the knees from the sharp rocks, and his gloves were so full of holes that they could not protect his hands any longer. Soon his hands had small cuts all over them, making every movement painful. Vincent paused to take a small drink of water out of his water bottle and wound some pieces of cloth around his hands. "Oh, God help me!" Vincent knew he did not have much strength left, not much chance of living. Then he saw it! "There is light at the end of the tunnel. But... it is not daylight. That does not make any sense. It is impossible," he thought. "That is not natural light, it is electric. Lamps and lanterns are hung on the walls of the tunnels!"

Vincent painfully kept going as he kept his eyes on the light ahead. "I feel like I am going as slow as a snail, just a couple of hundred meters will take me at least an hour." Then he thought, "If I could only see a golden eagle or a red deer... or hear the voice of Yen Yen!" In his mind he imagined what she would look like.

"Yen Yen told me she is from Taiwan, so she must be Chinese. Of course she is as pretty and fair as a princess or a doll, with black long hair that falls over her shoulders and back. But I will probably never meet her, too bad." These thoughts helped him pass the time and ignore the pain he felt in every part of his body. "At least my head has stopped bleeding," he thought as he tried to stay positive. His only desire was to reach the time machine and save the world from ruin.

用雙手和膝蓋爬行了兩個半小時之後，他的褲子早就被尖銳的石頭磨破了，他的手套也磨破了許多洞，已經無法再保護他的雙手。很快地，他的雙手被割出許多細小的傷口，讓他每做個動作都感到痛苦。文森停了下來，拿出水壺喝了一小口水，用一些布料纏住他的雙手。「噢，上帝，幫幫我吧！」文森知道他所剩的力氣不多了，存活的機率也不高了。接著，他看到了！「在隧道的盡頭出現了一道光。但是……那不是日光。這一點都沒道理。這是不可能的。」他想著。「那不是自然光，而是電子產品所散發出來的光線。竟然還有燈和燈籠掛在隧道的牆壁上！」

文森盯著前頭的燈光，繼續痛苦地向前爬行。「我覺得我前進的速度像隻蝸牛一樣緩慢，前進幾百公尺的距離得花上我至少一個小時。」接著他想著：「如果我可以看見一隻金色老鷹或是一頭紅色的鹿……或是聽到顏顏的聲音！」他在心裡想像著顏顏的樣貌。

「顏顏告訴我她來自台灣，所以她一定長得像中國人。當然，她一定跟公主或洋娃娃一樣美麗和白皙，還有著一頭自然地垂落在她的肩膀和背部的黑色長髮。但是，我可能沒機會見到她了，太可惜了。」這些想法幫助他渡過時間，讓他忽略了身體每一處的痛楚。「至少我的頭已經不再流血了，」他試著保持樂觀地想著。他現在唯一的願望就是能夠找到時光機，拯救世界不被摧毀。

Three days before Vincent was trapped in the tunnel, Dunkin, Lia and I were boarding the airplane at Taoyuan International airport. The evening before our flight we had been invited by Bi Bi to eat supper out. He knew the boss of a restaurant with an air conditioner in Hualien, where delicious seafood could be selected out of the big fish tanks next to the entrance. Bi Bi, Lia and I were eating shrimp, crab and fish with vegetables, nuts and rice. Lia added a generous amount of soy-sauce to her food. Dunkin looked at the menu and decided to try some corn soup, turkey and a medium-rare beefsteak with round baked potatoes and carrots.

Bi Bi commented jokingly, "I have eaten so much. The food was such a treat. Now I will have to go on a diet or I will get too fat!" For dessert we shared a chocolate cake and licked ice cream from cones to celebrate the beginning of a great adventure. We lifted our glasses of juice and beer as Bi Bi toasted to "saving the world," which was followed by another toast as I added, "and protecting Vincent."

On Thursday, December the nineteenth at seven a.m. we stepped into the airplane with mixed emotions. The flight was almost cancelled because of a strong typhoon. But the typhoon weakened and decreased, and finally turned into a regular storm, so our trip was given the go-ahead. Dunkin and Lia were so excited to fly in a plane they could hardly wait.

I, on the other hand, was a little afraid. "Did you consider the fact that the airplane is only made of a thin piece of metal that keeps us from crashing from a great height to the ground or into the ocean? How big is the chance that one of the engines stops operating or one of the wings breaks off?" I said nervously.

　　就在文森被困在隧道內的三天前，我、鄧肯和莉亞正在桃園國際機場準備登機事宜。搭機出發的前一天晚上，我們還接受畢畢的邀請一起出去吃晚餐。他認識花蓮一間餐廳的老闆，這間餐廳有冷氣，餐廳門口旁擺著大魚缸，可以從大魚缸裡面直接挑選美味的海鮮。我、畢畢和莉亞正在享用蝦子、螃蟹和魚，配上蔬菜、堅果和米飯。莉亞加了不少醬油到她的食物中。鄧肯看了看菜單，決定試試玉米濃湯、火雞肉和五分熟牛排，配上圓形的烤馬鈴薯和蘿蔔。

　　畢畢開玩笑地說：「我吃得太多了。食物太美味了。現在，我要開始減肥了，要不然我會越來越胖！」我們還一起享用了一個巧克力蛋糕作為甜點，也吃了甜筒冰淇淋來慶祝即將展開的偉大旅程。當畢畢舉杯說「敬拯救世界」時，我們也舉起手上的果汁和啤酒一同敬酒，接著我補充說：「還有保護文森。」大家又再次舉杯敬酒。

　　在十二月十九日星期四的早上七點鐘，我們帶著五味雜陳的心情踏上飛機。這個航班差點因為一個強烈颱風而被迫取消。但幸運的是，那個颱風逐漸減弱，最後轉變為普通颱風，所以我們的旅程得以開始。鄧肯和莉亞非常地興奮能搭上這班他們期待已久的飛機。

　　而我呢，反而覺得有一點害怕。「你們有沒有想過飛機只是由幾片保護著我們不會從高空墜落到地面或海面的金屬薄片所組成的？其中一個引擎停止運轉，或其中一個機翼分解的可能性有多大？」我緊張地說著。

Lia looked at me seriously, "What do you think will be more dangerous, flying a plane or being attacked by an angry wolf in the upper Swiss Alps?"

I replied, "OK, OK, I guess I will have to be ready for anything. Good thing Dunkin is coming with us." Lia gave Dunkin such a loving look that he turned around to hide his happy smile.

As soon as we had all found our airplane seats and closed our seat belts, Dunkin told us the plan that he had been discussing with Bi Bi the night before. "When we get closer to the mountain with the hidden waterfalls it may be right after sunset. Bi Bi is planning to fly far above us to be able to warn us of any possible danger, such as the wolf who may be guarding the time machine, or other unexpected events such as a landslide. He will be able to speak to me, in my mind."

We reacted as if Dunkin had just dropped a bomb. "What?" Lia and I both said surprised.

Lia said, "Do you have any other hidden talents you didn't tell us about?"

# The hidden waterfalls and a zoo

Dunkin silently shook his head and did not comment. He was not ready to tell all his secrets and opinions. Especially not in a public place like an airplane where everyone could hear what was said. It would take us at least sixteen hours to fly to Bern, Switzerland. After that it would take about seven more hours on foot to reach the hidden waterfalls. He reviewed these facts in his mind and thought, "I wonder where Vincent is now? Would he be able to survive for another twenty-four hours?"

莉亞嚴肅地看著我，「搭飛機或是在瑞士阿爾卑斯山上被一匹憤怒的野狼攻擊，妳覺得哪一個比較危險？」

我回答：「好吧、好吧，我猜我必須預先為任何事情做好準備。幸好鄧肯與我們一起去。」莉亞向鄧肯投以一個充滿愛慕的眼神，鄧肯不得不藉由轉身來隱藏臉上露出的幸福笑容。

當我們全都上了飛機，找到自己的座位並繫上安全帶之後，鄧肯告訴我們前一晚他和畢畢討論好的計畫。「當我們快要到隱藏著瀑布的那座山的時候，可能正處於太陽下山的時間點。畢畢會飛到我們的頭頂上空盤旋，以便在有任何危險發生的時候警告我們，例如那匹可能守護在時光機旁的狼或是其他無法預料的事件，像是山崩之類的狀況。他能藉由心電感應與我對話。」

我們驚訝的反應像是鄧肯剛丟出了一個炸彈一樣。「什麼？」我和莉亞同時驚訝地開口。

莉亞說：「你還有其他沒告訴我們的特殊才能嗎？」

# 隱藏的瀑布和動物園

鄧肯沉默地搖搖頭，沒有回答。他還沒有準備好要說出全部的秘密和想法。特別是在飛機上這樣的公共場所，任何人都可能聽到他們說話的內容。接下來至少還要飛十六個小時才會到達瑞士伯恩市。抵達之後，還要步行七個多小時才會到達那個隱藏的瀑布。他在心中回想了一次所有的事情，想著：「不知道文森現在在哪裡？他能不能撐過接下來的二十四小時呢？」

"Where are you? Are you alright?" Vincent could hear a voice in his mind. He knew this voice. His heart missed a beat and he felt butterflies in his stomach. "Yen Yen, I can hear you. That is marvelous. I can even hear you in an underground tunnel. I am not alone!" He was not totally sure if this was real or if he had died and was speaking to his guardian angel. Then he felt his sore hands and aching head. "It is real! You are really talking to me!"

I smiled to myself, "Vincent, please answer me. Are you OK?"

He was not sure how to answer as he didn't want to worry me, "I think I am. Oh, Yen Yen, I can hear water running down the rocks, the rushing water of a waterfall." Vincent had reached the end of the tunnel and his eyes were blinded for a moment by the electric lights that were hanging on the rock walls. "But... I am not outside at all. I am inside the mountain." He carefully stood up, trying to ignore his aching body. "I can see stairs cut out of the rocks." At that moment the sound of the rushing water became so loud that it was deafening. "Yen Yen, are you still there?"

The noise of the waterfall overpowered all other sounds and Vincent could hardly hear my voice. "Yes, but I have to go now. See you soon!" I replied. Then he lost contact.

「你在哪裡呢？你還好嗎？」文森的心中隱約聽到了一個聲音。他認得這個聲音。他的心跳開始加速，感到相當緊張。「顏顏，我聽得到妳的聲音。真是太神奇了。我在這麼深的地底隧道中還能聽得見妳的聲音。我一點也不會感到孤單了！」他不能百分之百確定這是真的，或是他其實已經死了，而他正在跟他的守護天使說話。接著，他感覺到手上的痠痛和頭部的疼痛。「這是真的！妳真的在跟我說話！」

我笑了笑，「文森，請回答我。你還好嗎？」

他不確定該怎麼回答，因為他不想要讓我擔心，「我想我還好。噢，顏顏，我在岩石下可以聽見水流的聲音，是瀑布的水流聲。」文森已經到達了隧道的盡頭，他的雙眼因為石壁上電燈射出的光線而漆黑了片刻。「但是……我還沒有走出隧道。我還在山裡面。」他小心地站起身，試著忽略身體上的疼痛，「我可以看見石頭砌成的階梯。」就在那一刻，水流的聲音變得很大聲，震耳欲聾。「顏顏，妳還在嗎？」

瀑布的聲音蓋過了其他的聲音，文森幾乎無法聽見我的聲音。「我還在，但我要先離開了。晚點見！」我回答。接著他失去了我的訊號。

Olec, after he drank the herbal liquid and changed into a wolf, was running in big circles from the hole that Vincent had fallen into, to the main waterfall inside the mountain. He was feeling restless and not at ease. After he had heard the sound of hundreds of bat wings moving in the hole, there had been total silence. "The boy is dead. He surely could not have survived this long even if he ate sand or small rocks to fill his stomach." Yet Olec's confidence was shaken and he tried to give himself courage by running at full speed. He had felt like this before.

Several months ago Olec, in the form of a wolf, had been hunting in the mountains when he had been attacked by a group of men in soldier uniforms, with guns. From an army helicopter they had shot him with a drug to put him to sleep. Then they had taken him to a zoo. It seemed to be part of a wolf protection program.

Olec was very angry when he woke up and found out they had put him in a large area with a fence around it, together with a female wolf. Then zoo keepers had thrown them rabbit meat covered with straw. "That looks terrible, I will never eat that!" he thought proudly. Posted on the fence there was an advertisement, which stated, 'Come and see the rare gray wolf from the Swiss Alps, the new hippo from Africa and the giant panda from China!'

　　喝下藥汁變身成狼的歐列克，正從文森掉落的洞邊跑回山內的隱藏瀑布。牠非常疲累且感到不安。牠聽到了數百隻蝙蝠在洞內振翅飛翔的聲音，接著四周重歸於完全的寂靜。「那個男孩死了。就算他吃沙子或小石頭來填飽肚子，他也一定無法撐這麼久。」然而，歐列克的信心卻動搖了，牠開始全速奔跑著，試著藉此給自己勇氣。牠之前也曾有過這樣的感受。

　　幾個月前，當變身成為狼的歐列克在山中獵食動物時，牠被一群穿著士兵制服的人攻擊，他們身上還帶著槍。他們從一台軍用直升機上用麻醉槍射牠，讓牠陷入昏睡。接著，牠就被帶往動物園。這些人似乎在進行一項野狼保育計畫。

　　歐列克醒來後，感到非常地生氣，牠發現自己身處在一塊空曠的地方，周邊圍著圍籬，旁邊還有一匹母狼。接著，動物園管理員丟給牠們一塊布滿稻草的兔肉。「這看起來真難吃，我絕對不會吃的！」牠傲慢地想著。圍籬上貼著一張廣告，上頭寫著：『來看看來自瑞士阿爾卑斯山的稀有灰狼、新來的非洲河馬和中國的大貓熊！』

Through the wooden fence he could see donkeys, zebras, elephants, lions and tigers. In the far distance there was a cage with bearded dragon lizards, and a pool with dolphins. "What can I do?" he thought to himself. "I will change to a man in thirty minutes. I need a plan quickly. I cannot become human in plain sight where everyone can see me." At last he decided to hide behind the biggest tree he could find and wait till the female wolf was not looking. Then back in human form, Olec raced as fast as he could to the fence and jumped over it, just as the female wolf tried to bite off his leg. Luckily she only tore off part of his pants.

"Stop!" he thought to himself. "I need to focus on the present. It feels like something is going wrong, but I don't know what." Olec shook himself from head to tail and pointed his wolf ears. He decided to check the time machine in its hiding place behind the main waterfall. "I am so intelligent, I am sure nobody will ever find it," he reminded himself with an evil laugh. "To reach the time machine a person would have to jump from one giant round rock to another. Only a wolf or large animal would be able to reach the other side. It will be impossible for anyone to do that unless that person is a superman!"

從木頭圍籬往外看，牠看到了驢子、斑馬、大象、獅子和老虎。遠處還有一個籠子，裡面飼養著龍鬚蜥，和一個養著海豚的池子。「我該怎麼辦？」牠想著。「我再三十分鐘後就會變回人類。我必須趕緊想出一個計畫！我不能在眾目睽睽之下變回人類。」最後，牠決定要躲在附近那棵最大的樹後面，並等到那匹母狼不注意的時候行動。變回人類後，歐列克用最快的速度衝到圍籬旁，然後在母狼差點把他的腳咬掉前，跳過圍籬。很幸運地，牠只有扯掉他褲子的一角。

「停下來！」牠想著。「我需要專注於現在。似乎有事不太對勁，但是我不知道是什麼事。」歐列克抖動全身，並豎起野狼的耳朵。牠決定查看藏在瀑布後的時光機。「我真是太聰明了，我相信沒有人會發現它的。」牠一邊想著，一邊邪惡地笑著。「想要找到時光機的話，這個人必須要從一塊大岩石跳到另一塊大岩石上。只有狼或者是大型動物才能夠成功地到達另一邊。任何人都無法做到，除非那個人是超人！」

# Time is speeding up

Bi Bi was listening to the latest news report on the radio, which he had borrowed from a friend, at eight o'clock in the morning. He had just gotten out of bed, brushed his teeth and washed his face. The broadcast on the radio was a discussion and review of current world events, and how they affected the culture and customs in many nations. "Violence and war have increased at an alarming speed," an important official said in an interview. "This year there have been more new wars between countries. But we are not only concerned about international wars. Currently there are also divisions within nations, cities and neighborhoods. People are arguing and fighting on the streets. Families have not been able to live in the same house peacefully. The question we have to ask ourselves is: Have people become worse than animals?"

"What has happened to teamwork, love and patience? Has the population of the earth gone crazy? Doctors have reported more patients are feeling hopeless as they cannot handle the time pressure. They feel that there is never enough time to do anything the right way. Not only that, but every day time seems to be speeding up. Companies are never able to produce enough products. Farms are not able to grow enough vegetables; as a result many people are going hungry." The news report finished with one final sentence, "Scientists all over the world, please work together to solve the problem!" Bi Bi turned off the radio when a music band started playing jazz music.

# 時間越來越快

現在是早上八點鐘，畢畢正用著向朋友借來的收音機收聽新聞。他才剛下床，剛刷過牙和洗過臉。收音機廣播正在討論和播報最新的國際事件，以及探討這些事件如何影響許多國家的文化與風俗。「暴力事件和戰爭的發生頻率以令人憂心的速度迅速增長。」一位位居要職的官員在訪談中說道。「今年有越來越多的國家爆發衝突和戰爭。但是，我們擔心的不只是國際間的戰爭。目前許多國家、城市和社區間也呈現不合和分裂的狀態。人們開始在街上彼此爭論和互相攻擊。許多家庭已經無法在目前的居所繼續和平地居住生活了。我們必須捫心自問的是：『人類是否已經變得比動物還糟了？』」

「我們的團隊合作、愛與耐心到哪裡去了？這個地球上的人類是不是已經發瘋了？醫生們指出，有越來越多的病人因為無法應付時間壓力而感到絕望。他們覺得時間永遠不夠用，手邊的事務永遠無法順利地完成。不只如此，每天的時間似乎過得越來越快。公司無法製造出足夠的產品。農田無法種植出足夠的蔬菜；許多人因此挨餓。」這項新聞的最後一句話是：「全世界的科學家，請共同努力解決這個問題！」當新聞結束，開始播放樂團演奏的爵士樂時，畢畢關掉收音機。

Bi Bi drank his glass of orange juice and ate some grapes and pieces of papaya, which he had bought in the supermarket yesterday afternoon. He looked at his watch. As stated in the flight plan of Dunkin, we would arrive at the airport in Bern, Switzerland at eleven p.m. and then would get some rest in a hotel close to the airport.

Bi Bi checked on his computer to see what the time difference was between Taiwan and Switzerland. He found out that Taiwan was seven hours ahead of the city of Bern. "That is perfect!" he thought. "That is so convenient for us. It means that the rescue team can hike and climb the Swiss mountain range by daylight by leaving in the morning, while I can fly above them as a golden eagle seven hours later Taiwanese time. At that time it is night in Taiwan."

"We are in Bern, we are here!" shouted Lia excitedly.

"Yes," I added, "Vincent, we are coming!" The airplane had just landed at the Bern airport.

But our happiness turned to worry when Dunkin looked out of the window of the plane upon arrival and saw crowds of people yelling and fighting. "What is happening?" he asked the person sitting beside him.

"It is a strike," the old man with a white beard answered. "Look at the signs the people are carrying. They want to find ways to increase their income, to earn more money for the work they do at the airport every day. They also want a better government to be elected."

Lia asked, "How are we going to change our money from American dollars to Swiss francs at the airport bank, so we will have some cash on us to pay for daily needs?"

　　畢畢一邊喝著柳橙汁，一邊吃著葡萄和木瓜，那些是他昨天下午從超市買來的。他看了看手錶。從鄧肯給的班機時刻表來看，我們應該會在晚上十一點抵達瑞士伯恩市的機場，然後會在機場附近的旅館休息。

　　畢畢上網查了查台灣和瑞士的時差。他發現台灣的時間比瑞士的伯恩市還要早七個小時。「真是太棒了！」他想著。「對我們來說很有利。這表示如果他們早上出發，白天就能到達瑞士那座山峰開始登山了，而我也可以在台灣時間七個小時後化身成一隻金色老鷹，飛往他們的頭頂上空。那時候正好是台灣的晚上。」

　　「我們在伯恩市了，我們到了！」莉亞興奮地叫著。

　　「對，我們到了，」我接著說，「文森，我們來了！」飛機剛降落在伯恩機場。

　　但是，當鄧肯從飛機窗外看出去時，看見了成群的民眾大聲喧嘩並互相攻擊，我們的欣喜之情立刻轉為擔憂。「發生什麼事了？」鄧肯詢問隔壁座位的人。

　　「是罷工，」蓄著白色鬍子的老人回答。「看看他們手上舉著的牌子。他們希望他們的收入能增加，他們每天在這裡上班，希望機場工作的薪水能提高。他們也希望能選出一個更好的政府。」

　　莉亞問：「我們要怎麼在機場銀行把美金換成瑞士法郎呢？這樣我們才有現金能支付在這裡的日常開銷。」

Dunkin shook his head, "We'd better do that in Bern. There are banks in the downtown shopping mall."

"But..." Dunkin questioned, "striking is not a reason to fight and get cruel."

The old man looked at him strangely and said, "Where have you been? Don't you know what is happening in the world? Everybody is arguing and fighting everywhere, peace can no longer be found. I think the world is coming to an end." The old man shook his head with tears in his eyes. "Life has no value anymore."

Lia and Dunkin looked at each other knowingly. They were both thinking the same thing, "Vincent has to get to the time machine and turn the key to slow down time. We are running out of time!"

All the passengers slowly and quietly exited the back door of the airplane and walked to the far end of the airport to avoid the mass of people who seemed to have forgotten why they were striking and carrying signs. Now crowds of angry people were just hitting anyone in sight.

At last Dunkin, Lia and I were able to buy tickets from the clerk at the bus station to take an express bus. Even though there was heavy traffic, we would soon arrive at a small hotel at the end of the local subway line, across from the central railway station where many trains arrived every day.

"That was scary." I said. "I am glad we got away from the crowded airport."

鄧肯搖搖頭說：「我們最好到了伯恩市再換。市中心的購物中心裡有銀行可以兌換。」

「但是……」鄧肯發出質疑：「罷工不應該是人們互相攻擊且變得如此殘忍的原因。」

那個老人納悶地看著鄧肯，並說：「你人都在哪？難道你不知道這個世界發生的事情嗎？世界各地的人都在爭論和互相攻擊，世界已經沒有和平存在了。我認為這個世界快要毀滅了。」老人含著眼淚搖搖頭。「生活已經沒有任何價值可言了。」

莉亞和鄧肯互相望著對方。他們心裡思考著同樣的事情，「文森一定要找到時光機，並且轉動鑰匙讓時間慢下來。我們快要沒時間了！」

所有機上的乘客都緩慢且安靜地從飛機後門離開，一路走向機場的盡頭，繞過這群似乎已經忘了自己為什麼要罷工和舉牌的抗議民眾。現在，這些成群的憤怒民眾見人就打。

最後，我、鄧肯和莉亞在巴士站買到了票，坐上了快捷巴士。雖然陸上交通壅塞，但我們還是很快地就抵達位於地鐵最後一站的一間小旅館，就在中央車站對面，每天都有許多班火車到達中央車站。

「真是太可怕了。」我說。「我很慶幸我們已經離開了那個擁擠的機場。」

Lia nodded, "Right, they should have hired a lawyer to work out their differences instead of fighting, or they should have voted for people to be their voice in the government." Before going to bed, she quickly sent an e-mail to her parents to tell them we had arrived safely and promised them to send a postcard from the local post office.

"We'd better get comfortable and go to sleep. We have a big day ahead," Dunkin said and softly started singing a song that he remembered from his childhood, "Over the mountains shines the sun, the people wake. The day has begun. The sky turns dark and the moon is bright. It is time to say goodnight!" As he turned around to look out the window, he quietly added, "Tomorrow will decide the future of the world."

# The race to the finish line

I was restless all night even though I drank a large cup of warm milk with honey before going to bed. I started counting the days and thought of all the possible events that could go wrong. "What if Vincent lost the key? What if..." Being half asleep all these thoughts became mixed up in my mind without being able to solve any problems.

"Enough!" I said to myself decisively. "I will get a towel and take a shower in the bathroom." After I had shut the bathroom door, I stepped on the mat to keep my feet from freezing on the cold floor.

The shower water started steaming when I heard a sound that was slowly but surely getting louder, "Yen Yen, are you there?"

I turned off the shower and covered myself with the towel to stay warm. Then I answered with a concerned voice, "I am. How are you?"

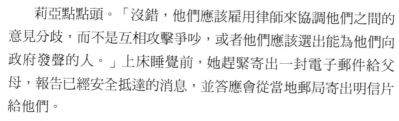

　　莉亞點點頭。「沒錯,他們應該雇用律師來協調他們之間的意見分歧,而不是互相攻擊爭吵,或者他們應該選出能為他們向政府發聲的人。」上床睡覺前,她趕緊寄出一封電子郵件給父母,報告已經安全抵達的消息,並答應會從當地郵局寄出明信片給他們。

　　「我們最好快點安頓休息。明天是個大日子,」鄧肯說著,並開始輕輕唱起他兒時記憶中的一首歌。「太陽照耀著山的另一頭,人們醒了。這一天也開始了。天色漸暗,月光明亮。該說晚安了。」當他轉身從窗外看出去時,他輕聲說道:「明天將會決定世界的命運。」

## 到達終點線的競賽

　　雖然我在上床睡覺前喝下了一大杯加了蜂蜜的溫牛奶,但我還是徹夜難眠。我開始數著接下來的日子,並思考著所有可能出錯的環節。「要是文森弄丟了鑰匙呢?要是……」在半夢半醒間,五味雜陳的想法在心裡翻騰著,還是未能理出個頭緒。

　　「夠了!」我果決地對自己說。「我要拿一條毛巾,到浴室裡沖個澡。」我關上浴室的門之後,踩上踏墊,讓我的腳不會碰到冰冷的地板。

　　當蓮蓬頭的水開始變熱時,我聽到一個聲音慢慢出現,越來越清晰,也越來越大聲,「顏顏,妳在嗎?」

　　我關掉蓮蓬頭並用浴巾裹著身體,讓身體保持溫暖。接著,我用擔憂的聲音回應:「我在這裡,你還好嗎?」

"I have a problem," Vincent replied. "The wolf, he is back. He hasn't seen me yet, but I cannot get out of my hiding place to get to the waterfall."

Around 5:30 in the morning I went downstairs and knocked on Dunkin's hotel room door. "Wake up! I need your advice!"

He slowly opened the door. "Lia, Lia, is that you?" Then he thought to himself, "I was just dreaming about her. I was a male swan and she was a female swan and we were swimming in a lake. How come she is knocking on my door?"

I laughed, "Dunkin, wake up please!"

He looked surprised and embarrassed, and then said politely, "Oh, I apologize for being confused, Yen Yen. Why are you waking me up so early in the morning?"

Dunkin quickly dressed and came out of his hotel room. "There is a small dining room at the end of this hallway. Perhaps we can sit there and talk."

"Dunkin, can you talk to Bi Bi in his dreams?" I asked. He was not sure what to answer. Actually he was able to talk with Bi Bi anytime and anywhere. It seemed like their minds were linked because their forefathers were 'dream catchers'.

But he didn't think he needed to tell me all his family's secrets, so he said, "Yes, especially when it is necessary."

I was pleased, "Great, that means you can give him a message from Vincent. He is close to the waterfall where the time machine is hidden, but he cannot get there. The wolf is guarding it."

「我遇到麻煩了，」文森回答。「那匹狼，牠回來了。雖然牠還沒有看到我，但是我沒有辦法離開目前的藏身之處前往瀑布。」

到了早上大約五點半時，我下樓敲響鄧肯飯店房間的門。「醒醒！我需要你的建議！」

他慢慢地打開房門。「莉亞、莉亞，是妳嗎？」接著，他自顧自地想著：「我剛剛才夢到她呢。我是一隻公天鵝，她是一隻母天鵝，我們正在湖裡游泳。所以她怎麼會來敲我的房門呢？」

我笑了出來，「鄧肯，請醒醒！」

他看起來一臉驚訝，而且有點不好意思，但之後還是有禮貌地說道：「噢，我為我的恍惚感到抱歉，顏顏。妳怎麼會這麼早叫醒我呢？」

鄧肯快速地換好衣服，從他的飯店房間走出來。「在這條走廊的盡頭有一個小飯廳。也許我們可以去那裡坐著談。」

「鄧肯，你可以在畢畢的夢裡跟他對話嗎？」我問。他不確定該怎麼回答。他的確能跟畢畢說話，不管何時何地。因為他們的祖先都是『捕夢人』，所以他們似乎心靈相通。

但是他不認為自己有需要把家族的秘密全部對我說，所以他說：「可以，尤其是在必要的時候。」

我很高興地說：「太棒了，這表示你可以傳達文森的訊息給他。文森離藏放時光機的瀑布很近，但是他現在沒有辦法接近那裡。那匹狼正在附近守護著時光機。」

Dunkin sat down on the yellow armchair, which was part of the furniture in the dining room and then asked, "So... why?"

I shook his arm. "I have an idea, Bi Bi can fly there as a golden eagle to bother the wolf and give Vincent a chance to get to the waterfall!"

Dunkin shook his head. "Yen Yen, it will not be that simple. I believe that we will need to be there altogether to assist Vincent. The wolf is not ordinary. He seems to be intelligent and willing to fight and die to protect the time machine."

Dunkin stood up to get a cup of hot coffee. "It is dawn. I wonder if there is already a buffet served for breakfast. I feel hungry. I guess it will not be available till eight in the morning. Oh, I can get something to eat out of the small refrigerator in my hotel room." After a couple of minutes he came out with a banana, some grapes and a box with yummy cupcakes. "Yen Yen, would you like some? I can think better with a full stomach."

I refused with a smile, "My stomach is not awake yet."

Then he became serious, "Vincent needs to wait, he cannot let the wolf know he is there. This is really important! You need to tell him now! There is a hidden trap right behind the waterfall that Vincent cannot overcome."

I looked at Dunkin curiously, "How do you know that?"

He looked at me with bright eyes, "That is a long story. We will discuss it over breakfast. Let's wake up Lia, pack up our backpacks and get ready for our mountain hike."

　　鄧肯坐在小餐廳的黃色扶手椅上，他接著問：「所以……為什麼呢？」

　　我搖了搖他的手臂。「我想到方法了，畢畢可以化身成一隻金色老鷹，飛去干擾那匹狼，讓文森有機會能夠到達瀑布！」

　　鄧肯搖了搖頭。「顏顏，事情沒有那麼容易。我相信我們必須一起去那裡幫助文森。那匹狼不是普通的狼，牠看起來相當聰明，願意為了那台時光機戰鬥，甚至不惜一死來保護它。」

　　鄧肯站起身倒了杯熱咖啡。「天亮了。不知道開始供應自助式早餐了沒。我已經餓了。我猜可能要到早上八點才有早餐。噢，我可以從飯店房間的小冰箱裡拿些東西出來吃。」過了幾分鐘，他拿著一根香蕉、一些葡萄和一盒好吃的杯子蛋糕走出來。「顏顏，妳要不要吃一些？我吃飽後的思緒會較為清晰。」

　　我笑著婉拒，「我的胃還沒醒呢。」

　　接著，他開始嚴肅了起來，「文森必須等待，他不能讓那匹狼知道他在那裡。這非常重要！妳必須現在就告訴他！在瀑布正後方有一個隱藏的陷阱，文森一定無法逃脫。」

　　我好奇地看著鄧肯：「你為什麼會知道？」

　　他用他那明亮的雙眼看著我說：「這說來話長。我們邊吃早餐邊說吧。我們把莉亞叫醒，整理背包，然後準備上山。」

After a four-hour hike we decided to take a break for lunch. "It is now twelve o'clock noon, let's not sit down in the open where anyone can see us," Dunkin said. "Sorry, we cannot make a campfire even though your toes are probably freezing." He admired us for our ability to walk for four hours straight in the freezing slippery snow and ice up the mountain sides. The mountain path had been covered up with snow and could not be seen as a result of stormy weather, and at times we had to use a thick rope, attached to the top of a big rock as a safety measure, in case our feet would slide.

I said, "I felt like I could hardly make it this far. Thanks for your help, Dunkin. I guess I should have trained harder in the gym. I am really thirsty now." I did not say anything about my sore legs and aching feet. "Could you pass me one of those blankets please?"

Lia looked at Dunkin with stars in her eyes. "This is the most wonderful adventure I have ever been on. I enjoy the action and the feeling of being on the edge of the world. I think I could live here forever! I would like something hot to eat though..."

Dunkin laughed, "The best is yet to come." Then he thought, "Or the worst, we may not survive." He sat down next to us and said, "I really need to tell you something." He felt a bit embarrassed and shy.

"Don't get scared when I start looking different. Remember Bi Bi can change into a golden eagle? I can become a red deer." Lia and I were speechless. We didn't know what to say.

Finally Lia said, "You... you are the red deer?"

I said, "But... wolves hunt deer. They are stronger."

經過四個小時的步行之後，我們決定休息吃午餐。「現在剛好是中午十二點，我們不要坐在空曠的地方，這樣很容易被人發現。」鄧肯說著。「抱歉，雖然妳們的腳趾可能都已經凍僵了，但我們不能生火。」他很佩服我們能在濕滑又冰天雪地的山中連續登山四小時。由於暴風雪氣候的關係，山路已經因為被白雪覆蓋而消失了，而且有時候我們還必須用套在大岩石上的粗繩索作為安全措施，以防我們的腳打滑。

我說：「我覺得我差一點沒辦法走到這裡。謝謝你的幫忙，鄧肯。我想我在體育館的時候應該要更努力練習才對。我現在真的很渴。」我還沒有說出我的腿已經很痠、腳也很痛。「你能不能遞給我一條毛毯？」

莉亞眼中帶著愛意看著鄧肯。「這是我經歷過最棒的冒險旅程了。我很享受這一切的行動，還有身處世界邊緣的感受。我想我可以永遠住在這裡！雖然我現在會想要吃些熱的東西……」

鄧肯笑著說：「最棒的部分還沒來呢。」接著，他想著：「或者應該說是最糟的部分，我們可能無法活下來。」他在我們身邊坐下，然後說著：「我真的需要告訴妳們一些事。」他有點尷尬和害羞。

「當我開始變得不一樣時，不要害怕。記得畢畢可以化身成為一隻金色老鷹嗎？我可以變成一頭紅色的鹿。」我和莉亞驚訝到說不出話來。我們不知道該說些什麼。

最後，莉亞開口：「你……你就是那頭紅色的鹿？」

我說：「但是……狼群可以傷害鹿，牠們比較強壯。」

Dunkin continued, "There is something else." We stopped eating our guavas and were all ears. "I am a protector."

I looked at him, "Of course, you are!"

Dunkin shook his head. "No, that is not what I mean. When there is danger and the people I care for could be hurt, then I become super strong."

Lia was not sure what to say. At last she could only think of two words, "Fantastic, marvelous!"

# Who will succeed?

At two o'clock in the afternoon Bi Bi was flying over the Swiss mountain range in the form of a golden eagle. With his eagle eyes he quickly noticed that the dark gray wolf was running out of the man-made tunnel on the side of the mountain, going south. In the meantime he could see Dunkin, Lia and I coming towards the east side of the mountain. This well-known mountain has ten waterfalls, which are hidden in the mountain and receive their water from the snow that falls on the highest mountains of the Swiss Alps.

"Oh, no!" Suddenly Bi Bi realized he would not be able to see anything that was happening inside the mountain. "Once they go inside the mountain to reach Vincent then I will no longer be able to help. They will be on their own." Alarmed, he told Dunkin and then flew in circles around the mountain. "At least I can warn them when the wolf comes back," he thought.

鄧肯繼續說著：「不只這件事。」正在吃芭樂的我們停了下來，全神貫注地準備聆聽。「我是一個守護者。」

我看著他說：「當然，你是呀！」

鄧肯搖了搖頭說：「不，我的意思不是那樣。當危險出現，而我守護的對象可能因此受傷時，我會變得非常強壯。」

莉亞不確定該說些什麼。最後，她能想得到的只有兩個字，「絕讚！」

# 誰會成功？

下午兩點鐘，畢畢正以金色老鷹的形態，飛抵瑞士阿爾卑斯山上。牠用銳利的鷹眼注意到那隻深灰色的狼正從山側的人造隧道中竄出，往南邊跑去。同時，牠也看見我、鄧肯和莉亞正往那座山的東邊前進。這座著名的山有十個瀑布，都隱藏在山中，這些瀑布的水都來自瑞士阿爾卑斯山脈最高的那幾座山所流下的融雪。

「噢，不！」突然間，畢畢意識到牠從空中無法看到山中的隧道內所發生的任何事情。「一旦他們進入山中找文森，我就幫不上忙了。他們就必須靠自己了。」畢畢感到不安，牠告訴鄧肯這件事，然後在那座山上盤旋著。「至少當那匹狼回來的時候，我可以立刻警告他們。」牠想著。

Dunkin, Lia and I went into the mountain through the tunnel on the east side and, after following several tunnels and walking up steps that were cut out of the inside rock wall, discovered the main waterfall, which was by far the biggest and the loudest. Vincent had given me directions to where he was hidden behind a big rock, so we could find him quickly.

"You are here!" Vincent called out. "I cannot believe it. It seemed like a dream." Then he said, "We don't have any time to introduce ourselves, we have to move now. The wolf has just left. But... I have to know, which one of you is Yen Yen?"

I felt both hot and cold at the same time and for a moment forgot about the time machine. "I am," I said softly.

Vincent turned to me and replied while looking in my eyes, "If we survive I will spend my life getting to know you."

Dunkin started speaking fast as we were running out of time, "Right behind the waterfall there are two very big round rocks, which form the entrance of the cave where the time machine is hidden. But there is a giant gap between the rocks. It is not possible for a person to jump from one rock to the other. The gap is wider than the maximum length that any human being can jump. Only animals can, such as a wolf or a deer." He looked at us, "I will have to change into a deer to get us across."

At that moment Bi Bi yelled at Dunkin, "The wolf went back into the tunnel!" Thirty seconds later the wolf appeared behind us.

我、鄧肯和莉亞從東邊的隧道走進山裡，走過幾條隧道、爬過幾個由山壁砌成的階梯之後，發現了主要的瀑布，這座主瀑布是這座山裡最大的瀑布，水流聲音也最大。文森之前已經告訴過我該往哪個方向走，才能到達他在大岩石後的藏身之地，所以我們才能很快地找到他。

「你們到了！」文森大叫。「我真不敢相信。這一切就像做夢一樣。」接著，他說：「我們沒有時間自我介紹，我們現在必須盡快離開這裡。那匹狼才剛走掉。但是……我必須知道，誰是顏顏呢？」

我一邊覺得冷，同時又覺得一陣熱，就在那一刻完全把時光機的事拋在腦後。「我是顏顏，」我輕輕地說。

文森轉身直視我的雙眼回答道：「如果我們能夠成功地活下來，我會用一生的時間來瞭解妳。」

由於時間已經不夠，鄧肯開始越說越快，「在瀑布的正後方有兩顆圓形的巨石，是洞穴入口，時光機就藏在那個洞穴內。但是在這兩顆巨石中間有一道非常寬的懸崖。一般人是不可能從一顆岩石跳到另一顆岩石上的。那道懸崖的寬度超過了人類所能跳的最遠距離。只有動物才跳得過去，例如狼或鹿。」他看了看我們，「到時候我得變身成為一頭鹿，才能讓我們所有人都過去。」

就在此時，畢畢對鄧肯大叫，「那匹狼回來了，牠進入隧道了！」三十秒之後，那匹狼出現在我們的後方。

Olec stopped for a second. He tried to decide whom he should attack first. "Who has the key?" he thought to himself. Then, "Why are there so many? It makes no sense to have two young girls here." At last he quietly moved back to hide in the shadows, hoping that we had not seen him.

Dunkin yelled angrily and instantly changed into a large brown bear that stood up straight. "I can smell a rat!" he said. He had heard a noise behind him and was ready to fight and pound the attacker. "Action time!" he thought. "It is now or never!"

Vincent, Lia and I had no second thoughts. We started running toward the waterfall.

The wolf saw what was happening and tried to block us from reaching the water that was rushing down.

"I command you to get out of the way. You are a worm not a wolf!" screamed Dunkin who, in the form of a bear, instantly took the wolf by the throat and threw him aside like a toy. Olec cried out as he hit the rock wall beside the curved mountain path. Then he was back on his feet. To Dunkin's surprise he turned around, went back and disappeared into a side tunnel. "The wolf is absent, run through the water of the waterfall!" shouted Dunkin. "On the other side is a big round rock, wait for me there. I will protect you."

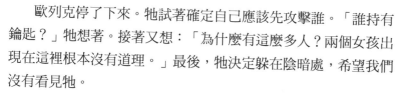

　　歐列克停了下來。牠試著確定自己應該先攻擊誰。「誰持有鑰匙？」牠想著。接著又想：「為什麼有這麼多人？兩個女孩出現在這裡根本沒有道理。」最後，牠決定躲在陰暗處，希望我們沒有看見牠。

　　鄧肯憤怒地大吼，並立刻變身成一隻直立站著的大棕熊。「我聞到鼠輩的味道了！」他說。他聽到自己身後有聲音，已經準備好要攻擊和重擊敵人了。「開始行動了！」他想著。「就是現在，機不可失！」

　　我、文森和莉亞毫不遲疑，立刻跑向瀑布。

　　那匹狼看見眼前發生的事，並試圖阻止我們到達向下沖刷的水流處。

　　「我命令你離開。你不是狼，你只是一隻蟲！」變身成熊的鄧肯大叫著，一把抓住狼的喉嚨，把牠像個玩具似的甩到一邊。歐列克撞上蜿蜒山路旁的岩壁後大聲哀號著。接著，牠立刻站了起來。出乎鄧肯意料之外，那匹狼轉身逃走，消失在另一側的隧道中。「那匹狼離開了，現在衝向瀑布！」鄧肯大喊著。「另一邊是圓形的巨石，在那裡等我，我會保護你們。」

Then there was total confusion. Vincent's, Lia's and my clothes were wet and our feet were sliding on the wet stones and rocks that seemed to be oily, trying to get to the other side of the waterfall. Vincent's head wound had started bleeding again and Lia and I had small cuts all over our legs. Then we saw Olec standing on the big round rock behind the waterfall. He had followed a side tunnel and had arrived on the rock before us. "Hello," he laughed, "you thought this was going to be easy. I will not move an inch. This is do or die, you will never reach the time machine alive."

# What is more important?

Dunkin, the large brown bear, raced after us and noticed at the same time that daylight was shining into the cave, behind the waterfall, from above. He only had one second to realize that holes in the rock wall, where the cold had contracted the rock, were letting in light.

Dunkin had acted too late. The wolf had picked Lia up by her leg and sneakily moved her above the giant gap between the two round rocks that formed the entrance of the cave where the time machine was placed. Vincent and I were powerless against the big wolf. "Come and get her, come and get her!" shouted Olec cruelly. "I will drop her and she will surely die. You failed. It is your fault. You should have been faster. You will regret this forever."

接著，發生一片混亂。我、文森和莉亞的衣服都濕了，我們試著衝向瀑布的另一側，但石頭和岩石又濕又滑，讓我們難以站穩腳步。文森受了傷的頭部又開始流血了，我和莉亞的腿上布滿了細小的割傷。接著，我們看到歐列克站在瀑布後的圓形巨石上。牠利用旁邊的隧道，趕在我們之前到達那顆巨石。「哈囉，」牠獰笑著說，「你們也想得太簡單了。我絕對不會離開。就算死，我也在所不惜，你們絕對無法活著到達時光機的。」

# 哪一個比較重要？

化身為大棕熊的鄧肯緊跟在我們後面，同時牠也注意到瀑布的後方有日光從上而下照進洞穴裡。牠只花了一秒就瞭解到，岩石因嚴寒的氣候而收縮，石壁上的洞因此形成，得以讓日光透進隧道。

但是鄧肯還是慢了一步。那匹狼已經叼著莉亞的腿，狡詐地將她拖到兩個圓形巨石中間的懸崖上方，這兩顆圓形巨石就是藏著時光機的洞穴入口。我和文森的力量無法對抗那匹巨大的狼。「來救她呀，來救她呀！」歐列克殘酷地喊著。「我會把她丟下去，她必死無疑。你們失敗了。這都是你的錯。你的反應太慢了。你會後悔一輩子的。」

Dunkin felt the anger rising in his body. He shook his head wildly, "No, calm down. I have to calm down and control myself." In his mind he thought a thousand thoughts, "Lia is the most important part of my life. She is dear to me. I care more for her than all the people in the world. I don't want to save the world. She is facing death, I have to save her!" Then he thought, "The wolf is evil. He tricked me. I have to focus on getting Vincent across the gap to turn the key in the time machine."

Lia was shouting and crying, "Dunkin help me, help me please!!" Then Dunkin, in the form of the brown bear, did the unexpected. Quick as lightning he told Vincent to get on his back, and then jumped across the giant gap to get into the cave.

Everything seemed to go in slow motion and several events happened at the same time. First of all, Vincent ran to the time machine and scared but brave, pulled out the key and turned it in the triangular lock. Then he started coughing and was so tired and weak that he had to lie down in the corner of the cave, to try to recover.

At the same time Dunkin called Bi Bi, "We need your help now! There are holes in the rock wall just behind the main waterfall. The holes are indicated by the light shining through. You have to fly through a hole and save Lia. The wolf is about to drop her into the giant gap. You have to catch her or we will never see her again. She will die when she hits the ground."

Lastly, the wolf could not believe his eyes. "How was that possible? The bear did not try to save the girl who would most certainly die!"

　　一股怒氣在鄧肯的體內升起。他大力地甩甩頭。「不，冷靜點。我必須冷靜下來控制自己。」他的心裡閃過一千個念頭。「莉亞是我生命中最重要的一部分。我很珍惜她。比起在乎全世界的人，我更關心她。我不想拯救這個世界了。她正處於生死交關的地步，我必須救她！」他轉念一想，「這匹邪惡的狼。牠在耍我。我必須專心，讓文森通過中間的懸崖，用鑰匙轉動時光機。」

　　莉亞邊叫邊哭，「鄧肯救我，拜託救救我！」接著，化身為棕熊的鄧肯做出了讓人意想不到的事。牠以迅雷不及掩耳的速度叫文森爬上牠的背，接著躍過中間寬闊的懸崖，到達藏有時光機的洞穴。

　　每個動作都像慢動作似的進行著，好幾件事情同時發生。首先，文森跑向時光機，他雖然害怕，但仍勇敢地拿出鑰匙，將它插入三角形的鑰匙孔中並轉動它。接著，他開始咳嗽，由於太疲累也太虛弱，他不得不在洞穴角落躺下。

　　同時，鄧肯在心中呼叫畢畢，「我們現在需要你的幫助！主瀑布後方的石壁上有許多洞。這些洞讓外面的日光透進來。你必須順著那些洞飛進來救莉亞。那匹狼要把莉亞丟下懸崖了。你必須接住她，要不然我們就再也見不到她了。她會掉下去摔死的。」

　　最後，那匹狼簡直無法相信自己的眼睛。「這怎麼可能？那隻熊竟然不救這個女孩，她命在旦夕！」

I looked at Dunkin who, still in the form of a bear, towered above me. He seemed even bigger and stronger than before. I was afraid to move and was as quiet as a mouse. I was praying that the wolf would change his mind and decide not to drop Lia. That instant the wolf opened his mouth and Lia was thrown into the giant gap yelling, "Dunkin, Dunkin!!"

In a flash a big bird flew down into the cave through one of the big holes in the rock wall. The golden eagle sped downwards into the deep gap and picked Lia up with his large claws and placed her safely on the rock next to me. Then Bi Bi's voice was heard above the rushing sound of the falling waterfall when he said frankly, "Everything will be fine, see you later!" and flew back through the hole into the open sky.

The wolf seemed to be frozen where he stood. "Was that golden eagle also speaking?" he thought confused. "I am dealing with magic, I am in big trouble."

Olec, the wolf, was about to run out of the mountain at top speed when the bear stood in front of him, "Not so fast, Mister. Whoever you are, you will not get away with hurting my loved ones and trying to bring the world to ruin."

我看著直立站在我身旁的鄧肯，牠還是一隻熊的模樣。牠似乎變得更龐大且更強壯了。我不敢移動，像隻老鼠一樣地安靜。我祈禱著這匹狼會改變心意，決定不把莉亞丟下去。就在那一瞬間，這匹狼張開了嘴，莉亞往懸崖掉了下去，大叫著：「鄧肯，鄧肯！」

一轉眼，一隻大鳥從石壁上的其中一個大洞飛進洞穴。這隻金色老鷹加速俯衝飛進懸崖深處，用牠的巨爪抓住莉亞，並把她安全地放在我旁邊的岩石上。接著，畢畢的聲音穿透瀑布的急流水聲，率性地說著：「大家都會沒事的，晚點見！」然後就從石壁上的洞飛出了洞穴，往廣闊的天空飛去。

這匹狼似乎全身上下都被凍結了，牠站在原地一動也不動。「那隻金色老鷹會說話？」牠困惑地思考著。「這些都是魔法，我麻煩大了。」

當這匹由歐列克變身成的狼正準備要全速逃出這座山時，大棕熊擋在牠面前，「別那麼快，先生。不管你是誰，你傷害了我的摯愛，並意圖將這個世界帶向毀滅，我是不會放過你的。」

Dunkin, the bear, hit Olec so hard that he crashed off the round rock into the waterfall and, after several seconds of uncertainly and dizzily sliding on the small stones, tried to run off again. The bear took him by the leg when he was about to get away. They pinned each other down and together they rolled onto the round rock, biting and bleeding. Then Dunkin saw how close they were to the giant gap and moved quickly by kicking the wolf off him and jumping backwards. Olec, in the form of the wolf, yelled loudly as he disappeared into the gap, with no hope of survival.

# Victory and travel

The bear jumped back across the gap and gently encouraged Vincent to ride on his back again saying, "Vincent, you did it! You turned the key so the time machine can slow down time to regular speed. The people of the earth will not only have enough time to feed and support their families, but they will also have time to understand and listen to each other. Everyone will be able to discuss disagreements and find peaceful ways to solve problems. Come now, we will join the others."

We all stood on the round rock behind the waterfall hugging and praising each other and feeling inspired, even though we were wet, tired and wounded. Dunkin had changed back to a slim, tall man who was holding Lia's hand and saying softly while looking into her eyes, "Please forgive me, I didn't know what to do. That was the most difficult decision I'd ever made in my life."

　　鄧肯變成的大棕熊猛擊歐列克，歐列克倒在圓形巨石上，並從巨石上跌進瀑布裡，因撞擊而感到一陣不知所措且暈眩的歐列克在小石頭上打滑後，牠試圖再次逃跑。正當歐列克要逃跑時，大棕熊咬住了牠的腿。牠們把對方撲倒，在圓形巨石上扭打成一團、互相撕咬著對方，雙方身上都血跡斑斑。接著，鄧肯瞥見牠們距離懸崖非常近，於是便將灰狼從自己身上踢開，快速向後方跳去。狼形的歐列克大聲嚎叫後便掉入深不見底的懸崖，沒有任何一絲存活的希望。

# 勝利與旅程

　　大棕熊轉身跳過懸崖，溫柔地示意，讓文森爬上牠的背，接著說：「文森，你做到了！你轉動了鑰匙，讓時光機將時間減速，回歸到正常的地球轉動速度了。地球上的人們不只能有足夠的時間來掙錢養家糊口，他們也有時間互相傾聽和瞭解對方了。每個人都能討論與交流彼此不同的意見，用和平的方式解決問題。來吧，我們去跟其他人會合。」

　　我們全都站在瀑布後方的圓形巨石上，互相擁抱、讚揚對方的表現，振奮彼此的精神，即便我們都已經全身濕透、疲累不堪且傷痕累累了。鄧肯變回了高挑、纖瘦的人類，他握住莉亞的手，看著她的雙眼，溫柔地說：「請原諒我，我當時不知道該怎麼辦。那是我這一生做過最困難的決定。」

Lia was shaking and had to sit down again as she was still in shock. Dunkin put his jacket around her shoulders and continued, "I thought I had lost you, but then I remembered the hole I saw in the rock wall and I told Bi Bi to come and save you. Thank God he caught you in time."

Lia said quietly, "I thought my life was over. I forgive you. I am so happy we all survived!"

I sat next to Vincent who was lying down and feeling weak but victorious. His head and neck wounds were still bleeding as the waterfall was spreading small drops of water all around us, so everything looked foggy and felt humid. I had put some blankets under and over him to try to keep him as comfortable as possible, but he was not able to get warm and his whole body was shaking. "Dunkin," I said worriedly, "we need to get out of here and fast! Vincent is getting too weak and the sun will be setting soon. It will only get colder."

Dunkin faced everyone and said, "First of all we need to get away from this waterfall and find a place in one of the caves to make a small fire to dry ourselves." Then he thought, "We have to be close to the entrance if we want to make a campfire, so the smoke can go out. There is no way we can go outside like this. We will freeze to death."

Suddenly I realized we had forgotten something important. "How are we going to get back to the city of Bern? Vincent is too weak to walk. We can't carry him, that's for sure."

Lia answered, "One step at the time, we need to dry up and we need to eat. Then we will be able to think more clearly." Soon we were sitting around a small fire close to the entrance of the cave and were eating all the food that was leftover in our bags.

莉亞不斷地顫抖著，因驚嚇過度而不得不坐下。鄧肯把他的外套脫下，披在莉亞的肩上，繼續說：「我以為我會失去妳，但是我想起石壁上見到的洞，於是我叫畢畢過來救妳。謝天謝地，他及時接住了妳。」

莉亞輕聲地說：「我以為我的人生會就此結束。我原諒你。我很高興我們都活了下來！」

我在文森身邊坐下，文森非常虛弱地躺在地上，但是仍流露出勝利的喜悅。他的頭和脖子都還在流血，瀑布的水不斷地噴濺，大家的視線都變得矇矓，感覺一片濕淋淋的。我在地上鋪了一些毯子，讓文森躺在上面，也幫他蓋了些毯子，試圖讓他舒服一點，但是他還是覺得很冷，身體也因此不斷地顫抖著。「鄧肯，」我擔心地說：「我們必須盡快離開這裡！文森太虛弱了，太陽不久也要下山了。到時候會變得更冷。」

鄧肯環顧眾人說：「我們首先得趕快遠離這個瀑布，並在這些洞穴內找到可以生火的地方，把自己弄乾。」他接著想：「如果我們要生火，我們必須靠近洞穴的入口，這樣煙霧才能散得出去。我們是不可能像這個樣子就直接去到外面的，我們會因為身體失溫而死亡。」

突然間，我發現我們忘了一件重要的事。「我們要如何回到伯恩市呢？文森過於虛弱導致他無法自行走路。我們絕對搬不動他的。」

莉亞回答：「我們一步一步慢慢來，我們先把自己弄乾，接著再填飽肚子。這樣我們才能更清楚地思考。」不久，我們在靠近洞穴的入口處圍著小火，坐成一個圈，吃著我們袋子裡僅剩的食物。

While eating the same thought went through our minds, "What will we eat tomorrow?"

A loud sound could be heard close to the entrance of the man-made tunnel. "What is that noise?" I asked worriedly. "Is that a large sheet of ice and snow sliding down the side of the mountain? That may block up the tunnel and we will not be able to get out."

Vincent lifted his head and said softly, "I know that sound. It is not snow and ice. It is a helicopter."

Dunkin nodded with a smile on his face, "I knew it was coming, but I didn't expect it to be that fast! Bi Bi, you are the best!"

Lia lifted her eyebrows and questioned, "You asked Bi Bi to arrange for a helicopter to pick us up? That must have been expensive." Then she walked over to Dunkin and put her hand on his shoulder while saying, "You are a genius, Dunkin, good thinking."

He now smiled broadly even though every part of his body was aching and sore, and he had many wounds from fighting with the wolf. "OK everyone, let's pack up and put out the fire. We are on our way. I will carry Vincent if you both take the bags."

The helicopter had landed on a flat area beside the mountain with the waterfalls. With the assistance of the helicopter captain, Vincent was carefully placed on blankets and jackets in the back. The instant we took off to fly to the nearest hospital in Bern, I realized we had forgotten something else. "We forgot something that is also important!" I said. "We were so concerned about getting back safely that we did not remember to make sure the time machine would not fall into evil hands again." Everyone looked up.

吃東西的同時，我們的心裡都想著：「明天呢？我們明天能吃什麼呢？」

在這個人造隧道入口處可以聽見一陣巨響。「那是什麼聲音？」我擔心地問。「那是一大片融化的冰雪正從山上滑下來嗎？那可能會封住隧道入口，這樣的話，我們就出不去了。」

文森抬頭輕輕地說：「我知道那個聲音。那不是冰，也不是雪。那是直升機的聲音。」

鄧肯笑著點點頭：「我知道直升機來了，但沒想到會這麼快就到了！畢畢，你最棒了！」

莉亞挑起眉頭並問：「你請畢畢安排直升機來接我們嗎？那一定很貴。」接著，她走向鄧肯，把手放在他的肩上說道：「鄧肯，你真是個天才，想得真周到。」

現在，鄧肯開心地笑著，雖然身體的每一處都因為與灰狼打鬥時受傷而又酸又痛。「好了，大伙們，我們收拾收拾，把火熄滅吧。現在準備上路回家了。妳們揹上全部的背包，我來揹文森。」

直升機已經降落在這座瀑布山旁邊的平坦處。在機長的協助下，文森安穩地躺在後座的毯子和外套上。我們才剛起飛，準備飛往伯恩市最近的醫院，我就發現我們忘記了另一件事。「我們忘了一件也很重要的事！」我說。「我們太擔心能不能安全地回家，都忘了確認時光機會不會再次落入壞人的手裡。」這番話讓每個人都抬起了頭。

Finally Dunkin answered, "That is true, but what can we do? We do not have the physical strength to block the way to the time machine."

Vincent's voice came from the back of the helicopter, "My father, he had contacts in the Swiss government. I could ask them to block the man-made tunnels, at all sides, as there could be safety concerns that the ceilings of the tunnels may fall down."

Dunkin expressed all our feelings when he said, "Good idea, Vincent, thanks, we are so happy to have you as part of our team!" One by one, we all felt the weight of the responsibility to save the world drop off our shoulders, and we slept all the way to the hospital dreaming of a better world where the population of the earth can live in peace.

# Home, sweet home

After Vincent was treated in the general hospital in Bern, he was able to go back home to the apartment building. His aunt was both crying and laughing at the same time, "You are home!" she said loudly. "But what did you do to yourself?" She quickly dried her hands on the hand towel and hugged him closely. "Get comfortable, I will get you something to eat. Please tell me the whole story." It took Vincent a long time to answer all her questions, till at last she was satisfied and he was able to get some sleep.

His thoughts returned to his new friends and above all to the special girl who gave him extra care during this dangerous trip. "Yen Yen, I still think you are an angel," he thought with a smile.

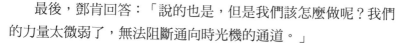

最後，鄧肯回答：「說的也是，但是我們該怎麼做呢？我們的力量太微弱了，無法阻斷通向時光機的通道。」

直升機後座傳來文森的聲音，「我的父親，他曾與瑞士政府往來。我可以請他們以『隧道有倒塌的安全疑慮』為名義，全面封鎖那條人造隧道的全部出入口。」

鄧肯臉上的表情說明了我們的喜悅之情，同時說著，「好主意，文森，謝謝，我們非常榮幸有你加入我們！」我們一個個都感覺到拯救世界的重責大任從肩上卸下了，前往醫院的路上，我們都陷入熟睡，做著一個世界變得更美好的夢，地球上的人都能享受著和平的生活。

# 家，甜蜜的家

文森在經過伯恩市綜合醫院的治療後，他終於能夠回到自家的公寓了。他的姑姑看見他喜極而泣，「你回來了！」她大聲地說。「但是，看看你自己！」她快速地用毛巾擦乾手，緊緊地抱住他。「好好休息，我來幫你準備些吃的東西。你一定要告訴我整件事情的經過。」文森花了很長一段時間來回答姑姑所有的問題，直到她滿意為止，文森才能夠去睡覺。

他的思緒回到了這些新朋友身上，最重要的還是那位在這趟危險旅程中給他額外照顧的特別女孩。「顏顏，我仍然認為妳是一個天使，」他邊笑邊想著。

Vincent remembered that he had promised me to come see me in Taiwan, as soon as he had recovered and was strong again.

"Vincent," I said to him when we were about to depart to the airport to fly back to Taiwan, "you told me when I first met you that you would spend your life getting to know me. I feel we are somehow linked together, even though I am not sure if we can still speak to each other in our minds when we are not together." Then with a laugh I said, "Of course cellphones are very convenient!"

Vincent gave me a hug and looked into my eyes, "Yen Yen, you and your friends have saved my life. There is no way I could have done this alone. I will keep my promise. As soon as I can I will come to Taiwan. We will soon see each other again."

The team received a warm welcome when they arrived at Bi Bi's little house on the hill. "Bi Bi, we are here!" Lia called loudly, hoping that Bi Bi was not asleep.

He instantly opened the front door and greeted us, wearing a vest and a pair of trousers. "You have finally arrived," he said cheerfully. "Come in, there is a lot of space to sit down now. You can sit anywhere in the living room."

Dunkin was speechless then he said at last, "You have actually cleaned your house. Wow, I can see the color of the sofa and the carpet now. The room is much bigger than I thought."

Bi Bi just smiled and said, "Tell me everything that happened, but first I will bring you some drinks and snacks."

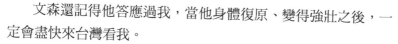

文森還記得他答應過我，當他身體復原、變得強壯之後，一定會盡快來台灣看我。

「文森，」當我們要出發前往機場飛回台灣時，我對他說，「我們第一次見面的時候，你說你會花一生的時間來瞭解我。我覺得我們之間有種連結，雖然我不確定當我們分開後，還能不能繼續透過心靈對話。」接著，我笑著說：「當然囉，手機很方便的！」

文森給了我一個擁抱，看著我的雙眼說：「顏顏，妳和妳的朋友救了我的命。我一個人是絕對無法轉動鑰匙拯救世界的。我會遵守承諾。在我復原後，一定會去台灣。我們很快會再相見的。」

當鄧肯和兩個女孩回到畢畢在山丘上的小房子時，受到熱烈的歡迎。「畢畢，我們來了！」莉亞大聲地叫著，希望畢畢沒有在睡覺。

畢畢穿著背心和長褲，馬上打開前門來迎接我們。「你們終於到了，」他歡欣鼓舞地說著。「進來吧，現在屋裡有很多空間可以坐下了。你們要坐在客廳哪裡都可以。」

鄧肯一開始說不出話來，最後終於開口：「你真的把家裡清掃整理乾淨了耶。哇，我現在看得到沙發和地毯的顏色了。房間比我想像中還要大得多。」

畢畢只是笑著說：「告訴我發生的每件事，但是，先讓我幫你們拿點飲料和零食。」

After having a lively conversation and answering many questions, Dunkin stood up and bowed to Bi Bi. "Uncle," he said, "you saved Lia from a certain death. She is standing in this room because you were there to catch her when she fell. I know I can never repay that. I am so thankful."

Lia gave Bi Bi a hug and said softly, "I have never been so scared in my whole life, but now I am here safe and healthy. You are wonderful."

Soon everyone was hugging each other and I said, "We need to celebrate! Any ideas?"

Bi Bi thought to himself, "There are other things that we need to talk about, such as the spiders and the white envelope that fell out of the ancient purple book." He walked quietly to the window and shook his head, "Later, this is not the time. Let's plan a celebration."

One month later both Lia and I received a text message from Dunkin on our phones. "Come to Bi Bi's house, we are going for a trip." Five minutes later Lia got another message from Dunkin. "I was thinking of hiring a ship, but actually renting a smaller boat was more practical. You'd both better bring your swimsuits. Do you know how to swim or row a boat? We are going for another adventure."

Lia and I looked at each other. "That sounds great," said Lia at last. "But I think we need some more information such as how long the trip will be, and where. What will we tell our parents?"

"Let's jog to Bi Bi's house, we need our exercise anyway," I suggested. Soon we were all gathered on his balcony and were sitting around a small table with a beautiful view of his garden.

在生動地描述和回答許多問題之後，鄧肯站起來朝畢畢鞠躬。「舅舅，」他說：「你把莉亞從死神手上救了回來，她能站在這裡，都是因為你及時地接住了她。我知道我無以為報。我非常感激你。」

莉亞給了畢畢一個擁抱，輕輕地說：「我這一生從來沒有那麼害怕過，但是現在我之所以能夠安全、健康地站在這裡，都是因為你。你真是太棒了。」

很快地，每個人都互相擁抱在一起，我說：「我們需要慶祝！有任何想法嗎？」

畢畢想著：「我們還有一些事情需要討論，像是從紫色古書裡跑出來的蜘蛛和掉出來的白色信封。」他安靜地走向窗邊，搖搖頭想著：「還是晚點吧，現在不適合。先來規劃一下該怎麼慶祝吧。」

一個月後，我和莉亞的手機同時收到了鄧肯的訊息。「快來畢畢這裡，我們要安排一趟旅程。」五分鐘後，莉亞又收到鄧肯的訊息，上面說：「我在想是否該租一艘大船，不過，租一艘小艇似乎更為實用。妳們最好帶泳衣來。妳們會游泳或划船嗎？我們又要踏上另一趟冒險之旅了。」

我和莉亞對視著。「這聽起來太棒了，」莉亞終於開口。「但是，我們需要知道更多資訊，像是這趟旅程會持續多長時間，以及這趟旅程的目的地。我們又該如何跟父母說呢？」

「我們慢跑到畢畢的家吧，我們仍然需要鍛鍊，」我提議。不久之後，我們聚集在畢畢家中的陽台上，圍著一張小桌子坐下，欣賞著畢畢花園的美景。

Bi Bi put some pizza and a salad with lettuce and tomatoes on the table and jokingly said, "You'd better eat lots. You will need all your energy for this trip we are planning."

Then Dunkin added, "By the way, Vincent will be traveling here from overseas. He will arrive in a couple of hours. Who would like to come with me to pick him up from the airport?" I jumped up with stars in my eyes, "Really? Of course I will go!" Lia thought it was a great chance to spend some more time with Dunkin so she happily agreed to come along. "Don't worry," said Bi Bi, "I have arranged everything with your parents. They have agreed to let you go on the trip."

# The celebration and surprises

After surfing the Internet on his computer, Dunkin had found a small island off the east shore of Taiwan called Green Island. The Internet advertisement described it as a beautiful place with a white sand beach.

"Fantastic!" said Lia. "That is just what we want. It will not be boring for sure. We can be sailors and sail the boat to the island, of course with the assistance of a captain." Both Bi Bi and I laughed.

Dunkin thought, "Great, she still has a sense of humor and a good imagination."

I added, "I wonder if there are whales and dolphins in the sea that we can watch?"

Dunkin checked his computer. "Yes," he said while at the same time thinking about playing frisbee on the beach, "although the whale watching season is from April to October. Nevertheless, we might still see some though."

畢畢在桌上放了一些披薩和加了萵苣及番茄的沙拉，開玩笑地說：「你們最好多吃些，我們待會計劃的旅程會需要大量的精力與耐力。」

接著，鄧肯繼續說：「還有，文森已經從瑞士過來了。他幾個小時之後就會到達這裡。誰想要跟我一起去機場接他？」我雙眼發亮地跳起身說：「真的嗎？我當然要去！」莉亞想到去機場的路上是一個能和鄧肯多相處的機會，所以她也開心地同意一起去。「別擔心，」畢畢說：「我已經跟妳們的父母解釋所有事情了。他們都同意讓妳們參加這趟旅程了！」

# 慶祝與驚喜

在上網搜尋資料之後，鄧肯發現在台灣東岸有一座小島，叫做綠島。網路上的廣告描述綠島是一個有著白色沙灘的美麗地方。

「太讚了！」莉亞說。「那正是我們想要的。這趟旅程絕對不會無聊。我們可以當水手，航向那座小島，當然，要在船長的協助下。」我和畢畢都笑了。

鄧肯想著：「太棒了，她的幽默感和想像力都還在。」

我補充說道：「我想知道，海裡有沒有鯨魚和海豚可以欣賞？」

鄧肯看了看電腦。「有的，」他一邊說，一邊想著還能在海灘上玩飛盤，「雖然賞鯨的季節是四月到十月。但我們應該還能夠看到一些。」

In the meantime Vincent had been flying above the clouds, comfortably seated in the airplane. He had been checking his watch every couple of minutes while thinking, "Why does time move so slowly now? Today feels like a million years. I cannot wait to see my friends again, especially Yen Yen. She is my Chinese princess." He looked at his watch once again.

Soon we were all together. Vincent was looking wide-eyed out of the car window at the Taiwanese scenery and the interesting mix of both modern and traditional houses and temples. "This island is so green and everyone seems so active," he finally said. "I think I will like it here."

I looked at him shyly thinking, "I hope you will like me too."

The next morning at six a.m., the fourteenth of February everyone was ready to board the boat. "I hope you brought some sunscreen cream and lots of water to drink," said Bi Bi. "It will be hot today, the sun is shining and there are no clouds in the sky."

Both Vincent and I answered at the same time, "We did." Then I continued, "We also brought lots of food for a barbeque and popcorn to have with our drinks later, and even some candles."

"I would like to introduce you all to someone who will be our guest during this trip," said Bi Bi unexpectedly. "This is my granddaughter, Miss Serena. I invited her to go on the trip with us. I hope that is alright with everyone." Before us stood a thirteen-year-old girl with short wavy black hair and a cute smile. She was wearing shorts with a long T-shirt and a colorful necklace.

"Hi everyone," she said frankly. "My grandpa told me the whole story of your adventure. You are all so cool. I would love to hang out with you!"

　　同一時間，文森已經在雲層上空舒服地乘坐飛機航行。他每隔幾分鐘就看一下自己的手錶，並想著：「為什麼現在時間過得這麼慢？今天就好像過了一百萬年似的。我已經等不及要再見到我的朋友們了，特別是顏顏。她是我的中國公主。」他再次看了看手錶。

　　不久，我們全都聚在一起了。文森坐在車裡，張大眼睛仔細看著車窗外的台灣景色以及現代與傳統風格混合的房子和寺廟。「這座島上一片綠意盎然，每個人似乎都非常有活力。」他終於開口說話。「我想我會喜歡上這裡的。」

　　我害羞地看著他，想著：「希望你也會喜歡上我。」

　　隔天，二月十四號早上六點鐘，大家已經準備好要登船了。「我希望你們都帶了防曬乳，還有足夠自己喝的水，」畢畢說。「今天會非常熱，太陽非常大，而且天空萬里無雲。」

　　我和文森同時回答：「都帶了。」接著我繼續說：「我們還帶了很多可供燒烤的食物，也帶了爆米花和飲料，甚至還帶了蠟燭。」

　　「我想要介紹一個人給你們認識，她會參與這次的旅程，」畢畢意外地說出這句話。「這是我的孫女，瑟琳娜。我邀請她一起加入我們的旅程。希望大家不會介意。」站在我們面前的是一位十三歲的少女，她留著短短的波浪黑髮，臉上帶著可愛的笑容。她穿著一件短褲和長版 T 恤，還配戴一條五彩繽紛的項鍊。

　　「嗨，大家好，」她大方地向大家打招呼。「我爺爺告訴我有關你們的冒險旅程故事了。你們真的是太酷了。我很樂意能加入你們！」

Lia turned to Bi Bi. "Do you have any other secrets?" she said with a cheerful smile.

"Well, I may have. I will tell you later when we are sitting around our campfire," replied Bi Bi.

"It is quite windy so the surf is big. I get seasick easily," Vincent commented while on the boat. He thought to himself, "This is a great excuse to hold Yen Yen's hand." He bravely took my hand in his and was pleased when I did not take it back. My heart was missing a beat and I had butterflies in my stomach as we watched the waves together.

"Oh no," I yelled suddenly. "Look, there are at least two sharks swimming close to our boat. What if..."

Dunkin walked up to us. "Don't worry, don't let them frighten you. I will be your protector," he laughed jokingly. "They will stay in the deep waters of the open sea. I don't think the sharks will come close to the shores of Green Island."

At twelve noon we arrived at the beach. Serena instantly ran to the sea and started dancing in the waves that were crashing on the beach. Vincent and I decided to go for a short jog on the wet sand, while Dunkin and Lia chose to play frisbee. Bi Bi was quite happy to sit on a towel on the beach and watch everyone play. He was surprised to see an elderly man giving horse and donkey rides. "This is the perfect playground, it just needs a seesaw and a swing," he thought to himself. His memories went back to the time when Dunkin was a wild teenager and Serena was a baby. "I was trying to keep them both happy. That was a hard job that took a lot of effort. Look at them now, they are having a lot of fun," he said softly.

　　莉亞轉身看著畢畢。「你還有其他的秘密嗎？」她愉快地笑著問道。

　　「這個嘛，可能還有。晚點我們圍坐在營火邊的時候，我會告訴你們的。」畢畢回答。

　　「現在風很強，海浪也很大。我很容易暈船，」文森在船上時這樣說道。他心想：「現在我有很好的藉口可以去牽顏顏的手。」他壯起膽子牽住我的手，而且很高興我並沒有把手縮回來。我的心跳瞬間加速，我們一起看海浪時，我也緊張得不得了。

　　「噢，不，」我突然大叫著。「看，那裡至少有兩條鯊魚游靠近我們的船，要是……」

　　鄧肯走向我們說道：「別擔心，不要讓牠們嚇著妳了。我會當妳的守護者，」他開玩笑似的笑著說：「牠們在海中會待在深水處。我認為鯊魚不會靠近綠島海岸的。」

　　在中午十二點時，我們抵達綠島海灘。瑟琳娜立刻跑向海邊，開始在拍上沙灘的海浪間跳起舞來。文森和我決定在潮濕的沙灘上慢跑一小段路，而鄧肯和莉亞則選擇玩飛盤。畢畢看起來相當開心，他在沙灘上鋪了一條毛巾，坐在上面，看著每個人享受著自己的活動。他很驚訝地看見一位老人提供騎馬和騎驢的活動服務。「這裡真是完美的遊樂場，就只差翹翹板和盪鞦韆了，」他想著。他回想起過去的歲月，那時鄧肯還是一個狂野的青少年，而瑟琳娜還只是一個小寶寶。「我那時候試著帶給他們快樂的時光。那很困難，而且花了我好大的功夫。現在看看他們，他們多開心，」他輕輕地說。

Dunkin and Lia first thought they would have a treasure hunt on the beach to look for crabs, wood or other things that may have floated to the shore. "It is like hunting for Easter eggs. Except crabs and pieces of wood will be our prizes," said Lia. But then they decided to build a sandcastle with a flag on top.

They hid some coins inside the castle because Dunkin said, "A sandcastle can be like a wishing well. If you hide coins inside, even if they are only one cent each, then you can make a wish."

He turned to Lia, "Maybe we can both say our wishes out loud. We already tell each other everything. We have no secrets."

Lia's ears turned red and as she looked down she thought, "This could be a little embarrassing."

Dunkin thought, "I have to tell her now, or I will lose my courage." Dunkin kissed her on the cheek as a gesture of love and said softly, "I wish we could get married." He quickly added, "In the future, of course!"

Lia looked shocked, "You must be joking, I am only eighteen years old!" Then she smiled and said humorously, "We will see." It was Dunkin's turn to have a red face. Lia quickly added, "OK, my turn. My wish is not a wedding, yet. I wish I will get to know you as well as I know myself. By the way do you know it is Valentine's Day today?" They both laughed and watched their sandcastle being washed away by the waves.

　　鄧肯和莉亞最初想要在沙灘上尋寶，找些螃蟹、木頭或其他可能漂上沙灘的東西。「這就像尋找復活節彩蛋一樣。只不過螃蟹和幾塊木頭是我們的獎品，」莉亞說著。但是後來，他們就決定要蓋一座上面插著旗子的沙堡。

　　他們在沙堡中藏了一些硬幣，因為鄧肯說：「沙堡就像許願池一樣。如果你把硬幣藏在裡面，就算只是一分錢，你也還是能夠許願。」

　　他轉身對莉亞說：「也許我們能夠一起大聲地說出我們的願望。我們已經告訴彼此所有事情。我們之間沒有秘密了。」

　　莉亞的耳朵開始紅了起來，她低頭想著：「這可能會有點令人害羞。」

　　鄧肯想著：「我必須現在告訴她，要不然我再也沒有勇氣說出口了。」鄧肯親親她的臉頰表示愛意，並輕輕地說：「我希望我們能夠結婚。」他迅速補充說道：「當然是指未來！」

　　莉亞看起來相當震驚，「你一定是在開玩笑，我才十八歲而已！」接著，她笑了笑，幽默地說：「我們等著看。」現在換鄧肯臉紅了，莉亞又說：「好了，換我了。我的願望不是一場婚禮，至少現在還不是。我希望我能更瞭解你，就像瞭解我自己那樣深。還有，你知道今天是情人節嗎？」他們都笑了，並一同看著他們的沙堡被海浪漸漸沖刷消失。

# More mysteries?

All six of us enjoyed the evening barbeque under the stars and were sitting around the campfire, singing and telling stories, while I played some beautiful music on the guitar. Even a local dog with his tongue hanging out of his mouth, came to sit next to the fire, to enjoy our company and to eat leftover bones that had fallen on the ground. "The moon and the stars make this evening heavenly," said Lia, after I had finished playing another song. "I cannot even imagine all this beauty being destroyed by that mad scientist who kept changing into a wolf."

Bi Bi added, "Even if he would have survived, the Swiss government would not have pardoned him for his crime. He would have spent a lifetime locked up in prison."

"By the way," Bi Bi continued while staring into the fire, which was slowly getting smaller, "perhaps our adventures have not totally finished. Even though the world has been saved from time running out, there are some other events we need to discuss. Remember when Alfred came to my house and gave me the ancient purple book, when I was just ten years old? Some things fell out of the book when Yen Yen opened it for us. I did not tell you at that time but I think you need to know now. A white envelope fell to the ground. Inside the envelope were two things, a diamond ring and a letter." Bi Bi instantly had everyone's full attention.

"Did you read the letter?" asked Dunkin.

# 更多神秘事件？

我們六個人就在星光的照耀下，圍著營火坐著，享受著夜晚烤肉的時光，唱著歌、說著故事，並聆聽我用吉他彈奏出來的優美音樂。還有一隻當地的狗，吐著牠的舌頭，靠了過來，坐在營火邊，享受著我們的陪伴並吃著掉落在地上的骨頭。「月亮和星星讓今晚就像置身天堂般幸福，」我彈完另一首歌之後，莉亞說著。「我無法想像這一切所有的美好事物都被那個會變身成狼的瘋狂科學家毀滅的樣子。」

畢畢接著說：「即便他倖存下來，瑞士政府也不會饒恕他的罪行的。他的後半生將在監獄中渡過。」

「還有，」畢畢眼睛盯著逐漸微弱的營火，繼續說著：「也許我們的冒險旅程還沒有完全結束。雖然我們拯救了這個世界，使這個世界不會因為時間加速而毀滅，但還有一些我們必須討論的事。還記得艾爾弗雷德在我十歲那年來到我家，給我的那本紫色古書嗎？當顏顏為我們打開它時，有些東西從書裡掉了出來。我當時沒有告訴你們，但是我認為你們現在需要知道。一個白色的信封掉到地上。信封內有兩樣物品，一顆鑽石和一封信。」畢畢立刻吸引了大家的注意力。

「你讀那封信了嗎？」鄧肯問。

"It is very strange," said Bi Bi, "A message was written on the outside. It said, 'This letter cannot be opened till June or July, 2019'. That is in a couple of months. I tried to see if I could open it, but it was impossible."

Dunkin interrupted, "You also need to tell them about the spiders. I hope no one here is afraid of spiders."

Both Lia and I were alarmed. "Why?" we asked at the same time.

"Well, a couple of small black spiders also fell out of the book and ran under Bi Bi's sofa, but they may be normal spiders that just happened to live in the book. I am not sure. We have no idea where they are now," Dunkin said softly. The fire had gone out by the time we finished our conversation and we were all sitting in the dark.

"Let's go back to our hotel and we may dream about it," Bi Bi suggested with a big smile. "I have the feeling our lives together will always be exciting and mysterious."

~To Be Continued~

「這封信非常奇怪，」畢畢說。「信的外層寫了一個訊息，上面說：『這封信必須等到 2019 年 6 月或 7 月才能打開。』距離這個時間還有幾個月。我試過提前打開它，但是沒有成功。」

鄧肯打岔：「你還需要告訴他們關於蜘蛛的事情。我希望在座所有的人都不怕蜘蛛。」

莉亞和我開始感到不安。「為什麼？」我們同時開口問道。

「這個嘛，還有幾隻黑色的小蜘蛛也從書裡掉了出來，並鑽進畢畢的沙發底下，但是牠們可能就只是一般的蜘蛛，只是剛好住在那本書裡面而已。但是我不敢確定。我們不知道牠們現在跑去哪了，」鄧肯輕輕地說。當我們結束談話時，營火早已熄滅，所以我們所有人全都坐在一片漆黑之中。

「我們回去飯店吧，也許我們會夢到這件事，」畢畢提議，並綻放一個大大的笑容。「我有預感，我們的生活會一直充滿驚喜和神秘。」

～未完待續～

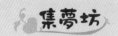

# 幻金天騎：尋找神秘的呼喚者

出版者●集夢坊
作者●Vera Martin
策劃者●李政鴻
譯者●中華翻譯社
印行者●全球華文聯合出版平台
總顧問●王寶玲
出版總監●歐綾纖
副總編輯●陳雅貞
責任編輯●林詩庭
美術設計●陳君鳳
內文排版●王芋崴

國家圖書館出版品預行編目（CIP）資料

幻金天騎：尋找神秘的呼喚者／Vera Martin 著
-- 新北市：集夢坊出版，采舍國際有限公司發行
2020.7　　面；　　公分
中英對照
譯自：Golden Skyrider : The Search for the
　　　Mysterious Caller
ISBN 978-986-96132-9-3（平裝）
1.英語　2.讀本

805.18　　　　　　　　　　　　　　109005355

台灣出版中心●新北市中和區中山路2段366巷10號10樓
電話●(02)2248-7896　　　　傳真●(02)2248-7758
ISBN●978-986-96132-9-3　　出版日期●2020年10月三版二刷

郵撥帳號●50017206采舍國際有限公司（郵撥購買，請另付一成郵資）
全球華文國際市場總代理●采舍國際 www.silkbook.com
地址●新北市中和區中山路2段366巷10號3樓
電話●(02)8245-8786　　　　傳真●(02)8245-8718

全系列書系永久陳列展示中心
新絲路書店●新北市中和區中山路2段366巷10號10樓　　電話●(02)8245-9896
新絲路網路書店●www.silkbook.com　　　　華文網網路書店●www.book4u.com.tw

跨視界‧雲閱讀 新絲路電子書城 全文免費下載 silkbook〇com
新‧絲‧路‧網‧路‧書‧店

本書係透過全球華文聯合出版平台（www.book4u.com.tw）印行，並委由采舍國際有
限公司（www.silkbook.com）總經銷。採減碳印製流程，碳足跡追蹤，並使用優質中
性紙（Acid & Alkali Free）通過綠色環保認證，最符環保要求。